ALLAN AHLBERG

The Boyhood of Burglar Bill

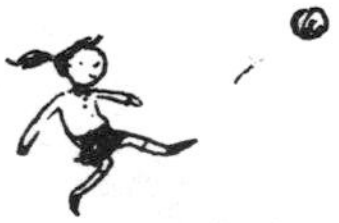

PUFFIN

PUFFIN BOOKS

Published by the Penguin Group
Penguin Books Ltd, 80 Strand, London WC2R 0RL, England
Penguin Group (USA) Inc., 375 Hudson Street, New York, New York 10014, USA
Penguin Group (Canada), 90 Eglinton Avenue East, Suite 700, Toronto, Ontario, Canada M4P 2Y3
(a division of Pearson Penguin Canada Inc.)
Penguin Ireland, 25 St Stephen's Green, Dublin 2, Ireland (a division of Penguin Books Ltd)
Penguin Group (Australia), 250 Camberwell Road, Camberwell, Victoria 3124, Australia
(a division of Pearson Australia Group Pty Ltd)
Penguin Books India Pvt Ltd, 11 Community Centre, Panchsheel Park, New Delhi – 110 017, India
Penguin Group (NZ), 67 Apollo Drive, Mairangi Bay, Auckland 1310, New Zealand
(a division of Pearson New Zealand Ltd)
Penguin Books (South Africa) (Pty) Ltd, 24 Sturdee Avenue, Rosebank, Johannesburg 2196, South Africa

Penguin Books Ltd, Registered Offices: 80 Strand, London WC2R 0RL, England

penguin.com

Published 2006
1

Set in Monotype Baskerville by
Palimpsest Book Production Limited, Grangemouth, Stirlingshire
Made and printed in England by Clays Ltd, St Ives plc

British Library Cataloguing in Publication Data
A CIP catalogue record for this book is available from the British Library

ISBN-13: 978-0-141-38284-5

The Players

Boys

Spencer Sorrell
Ronnie Horsfield
Tommy Ice Cream
Tommy Pye
Joey Skidmore
Trevor Darby
Malcolm Prosser
Patrick Prosser
Graham Glue
Arthur Toomey
Wyatt

Other Boys

Amos
Vincent Loveridge

Dogs

Archie
Dinah
Rufus
Sadie and six pups,
including Ramona

Girls

Edna May Prosser
Brenda Bissell
Monica Copper

Teachers

Mr Cork
Mr Reynolds
Miss Palmer
Mrs Belcher
Mrs Harris

Barbers

Mr Cotterill

Dignitaries

Alderman and
Mrs Haywood

Plus assorted parents, shopkeepers, park-keepers, bus conductors, referees and linesmen, not forgetting Mrs Moore, old man Cutler, Ray Barlow himself, too many Toomeys. Oh yes, of course, and me.

Part One

I

One-armed Man, Three-legged Dog

The best and worst times of my life occurred, I truly believe, before I was twelve years old. It was another world in those days: terraced houses, wash houses, communal yards. Our lavatory was a brick-built gloomy box at the end of the garden. I got a good part of my education – world affairs, showbiz gossip – from torn squares of newspaper stuck out there on a nail behind the door. The streets were full of kids and empty of cars; the park, an orderly and enormous wilderness. Everything was urgent – vivid – outlined in fire at times. The world did not merely spin in those days, it went up and down like a roller-coaster.

Mr Cork was a madman. He had a wide flat face like a garden spade, and one arm. He often carried a cricket stump. If you didn't know the answer to some question or other, he would hammer your desk – bang! – and jump you out of your skin. He had this gravelly voice. 'Ahlberg,' he'd say. 'C'mere.' He was a teacher you see, supposed to be. Emergency-trained, for lion-taming, Joey Skidmore reckoned. There was a shortage of teachers after the war and more than a few of them had bits missing.

He was cunning too. You might think you knew it was coming, that cricket-stump trick, and grit your teeth determined *not* to jump. But he'd move on along the aisle, allowing some kid just time enough to breathe his sigh of relief, then quick dart back and – wallop! A heavy man he was, but light on his feet.

Mr Cork taught craft to the boys when the girls were having needlework with Miss Palmer. Also once a week on a Wednesday he'd march the boys, about sixty-six of us, out of the school gates, along Rood End Road, down Oldbury Road, across the Birmingham Road and into Guest, Keen & Nettlefold's sports ground for football in the football season, cricket in the cricket. And that was how it started.

Sixty-six boys, more or less, two footballs, two sets of shirts, one madman and a whistle. This was how things were organized. Mr Cork took the first and second teams on the top pitch. It had goalposts, nets, even corner flags sometimes. They played a proper match. Mr Cork, with his trousers tucked in his socks and his empty sleeve flapping, ran up and down kicking wildly at the ball from time to time, yelling at the kids. Coaching, he called it. This went on for a whole afternoon.

Meanwhile, down on the bottom pitch forty-four boys organized themselves into two warring factions and played their own game. No referee, no kit and pitch markings you could hardly see. It was like one of those historical events you get on TV where one half of a village tries to move a pumpkin or something up the hill and the other half tries to stop them. The groundsman stored his rollers along one side of this supposed pitch. There was a brook and a seasonal swamp behind one goal, scrap metal, huge coils of wire, containers full of toxic waste, I wouldn't be surprised. But maybe I'm exaggerating.

The weather had little influence on Mr Cork. In wind and rain, snow and ice, if it was Wednesday we went. Mud never bothered him at all. (I wonder now though what *his* mother, or wife maybe, made of it.) Afterwards we'd troop back up the hill to school, kids peeling off when we passed their streets, like an army of zombies or *Flash Gordon and the Claymen*.

*

One Wednesday, a dry and sunny day as it happened, the three of us – Spencer, Ronnie and me – left Mr Cork's retreating column outside Milward's. Ronnie picked up his gran's copy of the local paper, Spencer bought a liquorice pipe. We stood around admiring the contents of Milward's window.

'Bags I that *Rupert* annual,' Spencer said. 'Bags I . . .'

Ronnie read the paper. There was a picture of a pools winner on the front page; the Mayor and Mayoress having tea in an old people's home. And on the back an account of Oldbury Town's latest fixture and an entrance form for the Coronation Cup.

'Says here, the Cubs've gotta team up . . .'

Spencer peered over Ronnie's shoulder.

'. . . and the Boys' Brigade.'

Spencer made no comment. He broke off a bit of his pipe and pushed it into Ronnie's mouth. I stared at my reflection in the window, hair on end as usual like a cockatoo. Mrs Milward glared back at us and shooed us away. She judged we were up to something. Milward's had more stuff pinched than they sold, according to her. I took a kick at a cigarette packet on the pavement; we moved off. On the allotments, old man Cutler in his off-white painter's overalls and his pork-pie hat was tending his bonfire, smoke billowing across the road.

'We could get a team up,' Spencer said.

The next morning in assembly Mr Reynolds talked to the whole school about boys peeing up the wall in the outside toilets, kids frothing up their milk with straws, kids kicking balls deliberately from the boys' playground into the girls' and infants' playground, Jesus and the Coronation Cup. Rood End Primary would enter two teams, he said. The rest of us, he was sure, would want to come along and support the teams and, by implication, the entire royal family. Preliminary rounds would be played . . . the final was on . . . dates, times, places. Then, as Mrs Belcher struck up her 'walking nicely music' and we were leaving, Mr Reynolds saw fit to speak again.

'Toomey – stop that. See me afterwards.'

'Which one, Sir?' said a voice.

'Er . . . Brian.'

'See all of 'em, Sir!'

'Who said that?'

There were three Toomeys in the hall on that occasion; could have been four. Maurice Toomey was away working for his dad, or up at the juvenile court, more like.

At playtime Spencer and I played marbles with Joey Skidmore and lost. The Purnells' three-legged dog, Archie, got under the gates and raced around the playground for a while, creating havoc. Archie was a wonder dog in all our eyes. Nearly a year ago he had got run over. They found his foot in the street but the rest of him ran off. Mr Purnell mourned for a while; Mrs Purnell offered to beat the motorcyclist up or at least wreck his bike. Then, lo and behold, a fortnight later back came Archie. Subsequently, he treated the Purnells with disdain, steered clear of traffic and was generally adopted by the neighbourhood. He could get a bone anywhere.

Lining up after playtime, Spencer and I compared our losses. Ronnie claimed to have been peeing up the outside-toilet walls in a competition organized by Amos. A ball came flying over the wall *from* the girls' and infants' playground, which raised a cheer. And Ronnie said, 'We could y'know.'

'What?'

'What?'

'Get a team up.'

2

The Coronation Cup

Mrs Glue peered suspiciously at us, the door open just enough to accommodate her head.

'Graham's out.'

'But we've just seen him come in, Mrs Glue,' said Spencer in his politest voice.

'Oh, well he's in then.'

Whereupon another voice from inside. 'And in he's stoppin'.'

Mr Glue, that was.

'Couldn't Graham come out and . . .' I didn't give up that easily.

'He's havin' his tea.'

'After his tea?'

'He's helpin' his dad.'

Voice from inside. ''E's no help.'

At which point Graham's face, with its shock of almost-white hair, squeezed into view under his mother's arm. Somehow, without actually speaking, he indicated that he would see us later up the park with his boots. He'd spotted me with mine and Spencer with the ball.

After Graham we tried Joey Skidmore and he was out, Malcolm Prosser and he was out, and Trevor Darby and he was out. Gone for a haircut, his sister said. So off we trooped to Cotterill's.

Trevor was kneeling up in the chair when we got there. We could see him through the window. Mr Cotterill, with a cigarette in his mouth and a cup of tea at his elbow, was running the clippers up and over the top of Trevor's head. The radio was blaring out. Trevor's mother was in there, clutching her handbag and looking anxious. She instructed Mr Cotterill in the finer points of hairstyling she required for her beloved son. Mr Cotterill adjusted his hearing aid and nodded. His eyes behind the thick lenses of his glasses looked like little blue fish swimming around. Yes, and one thing more to complete the picture: his hand – with scissors, clippers, sometimes even an open razor in it – ever so slightly shook.

Trevor got down from the chair and, though more or less bald, seemed cheerful enough. He was unable to join us, however. Off to the hospital with his mum to see his gran. (And show her where his hair had been!) All this was happening on the

Friday after we had read and heard about the Coronation Cup on the Wednesday and Thursday. We were getting a team up.

It was the end of March now, 1953. The Coronation of Queen Elizabeth II would take place in June, with half the street crowded into the Skidmores' watching it all on a nine-inch black-and-white TV. The cup itself (the main event, in our eyes) was for under-twelves; there was an under-sixteens one as well, as I recall. It was assumed that mostly schools would enter, plus boys' clubs, scout groups and so on. Matches would be played throughout April on a knockout basis. The final to be held at Accles & Pollock's sports ground, with its superior facilities and proper stand, presentation of medals by Ray Barlow himself, on the 22nd of April. The entrance fee was five bob, 25p in today's money.

Later that evening we sat in the park sheds watching a shower of rain go bouncing across the pond: Graham Glue, Joey Skidmore, Spencer, Ronnie and me.

'So who else have we got?' said Joey.

'Trev'll play,' I said.

'My cousin's a good 'un,' Graham said.

'How about Prosser?' said Ronnie.

'He'll only play if his brother plays,' said I. 'His brother's useless.'

The Prosser brothers were twins and, aside from their footballing skills, hard to tell apart.

'I know who we should get,' said Joey.

'Who?'

'Tommy Pye.'

'Tommy Pye, he's only seven!'

'Have you seen him play?'

'He's a midget.'

'Have you *seen* him?'

On the way home, we went round to Tommy's, the whole lot of us. But his mother said he was in bed. Back in the street, we could see his little face up at the bedroom window. He gave us a wave.

We split up then. Eventually, Spencer and I made our way to Cemetery Road. He and I were near neighbours. At the top of the road we passed a couple of the older Toomeys, Albert and Rufus, lounging around outside the Malt Shovel. They took offence at Spencer as we went by. They judged him to be a snob on account of his collar and tie. Albert accused us of looking at them. We kept going. At a safe distance I yelled defiance, partly because Monica Copper, a girl I secretly admired, was out in her garden. The Toomeys came running, but soon gave up. We had too good a lead.

Spencer was worried, even before the Toomeys. He had missed his accordion lesson. What could he tell his mother?

'Tell her you asked a man in the park and he told you the wrong time,' I offered. 'Tell her you ran from a horsefly.'

My mum was in the yard beating the daylights out of a rug. A shaft of light from the open doorway illuminated the scene. Half the kitchen furniture was out there. She was laying lino. I made myself a sugar sandwich and, when the coast was clear of Toomeys, took Dinah for a walk.

3

The Strong Man's Daughter

> We alight at Oldbury, in Worcestershire, a place of smother amid smother, and, on leaving the station, can count seventy-nine furnace and factory chimneys without turning round, all of which pour forth their cloudy contributions, varied by the blue and yellow smoke of copper-works, while noises resound afar.
>
> Walter White, *All Round the Wrekin* (1860)

My mother loved me. Though she hit me with a broom handle, she loved me. Though she locked me in the coal-shed sometimes, still she did. I know this now. She was, I remember, angry and strong. I'd come home from school and find she'd moved a wardrobe. There were startling rearrangements of the entire house every few months. Also we seemed to move house – exchange houses – all the time. Before I was eight I had been to three different schools and made no friends in any of them.

My mother was a bit mad. She roamed the streets in her nightgown sometimes, at two in the morning – in the wind and rain, it didn't matter – till Dad caught up with her and brought her home. In all the photographs I have of her, not many, she's frowning, squinting at the sun whether it was out or not.

But still she loved me. She wrapped a hot plate from the oven in a towel and put it in my bed on winter nights. She took my side when a neighbour accused us (rightly, as it happened) of breaking up her fence and stealing it for bonfire night. She worked all hours and spent the modest sums she earned mostly on me.

We moved to Cemetery Road when I was nine and a half, having arrived from Stone Street and before that Birchfield Lane and before that . . . I don't remember. After the war Mum led us on a zigzag course across the town, in one side and out the other. It was the latest step in her secret plan (not so secret, really, I just never thought to ask). That town, it was a sort of Venice; you could not get in or out without crossing a canal. It was a town of industrial noise and fog. In those days I could have told you where I was blindfold, just from the various and famous factory smells.

When I recall my mum, I often picture her as *Pansy Potter, the Strong Man's Daughter* in the *Dandy*, out-removing the removal men with her mighty forearms. She had, as they say, an arm like a leg. Her anger, though, was like a compass needle that all too often swung to violence. This was not all bad. On one occasion the Toomeys chased us, me and Spencer, down the entry. We barricaded ourselves in the wash house, where they discovered us and banged on the door. Mum came out and drove them off with her bare hands. Only then, losing her Boadicea image somewhat, she did the Toomeys' work for them and clouted me herself.

My mother had a tiny birthmark high up on her forehead, almost in her hair. It resembled a bunch of grapes. She was partially deaf in one ear from a blow to the head received in childhood from *her* mother. She had her own distinctive smell: washing and ironing, the minty aroma of her medicine, and Bible scent-cards.

Bits of my mother, aspects or versions of her, have appeared in other books of mine over the years. She was the mother, for instance, in some of the *Please Mrs Butler* (1983) poems:

Our mother is a detective.
She is a great finder of clues.

That was her.

I did a bad thing once.
I took this money from my mother's purse.

Yes, Mum again – her purse – and me. Anyway, here she is, my old mum, with a part to play in *this* story. She moved me into it, as I have said, and will move me out when the time comes.

4

Squealing Pigs and Too Many Toomeys

Saturday morning was a scramble. By lunchtime we had three-quarters of a team and had handed in our entrance form plus five-bob fee at the town hall. The money was mostly mine and Spencer's at this stage. I earned money doing jobs for Mrs Moore, collecting pennies on empty beer and pop bottles taken back to the Malt Shovel, and helping Stan Pike on occasion with his paper round. Spencer got pocket money.

We needed a name for our team to put on the form, and the name and address of our 'club/school/team' secretary. Spencer put his dad's name down for that. As for the team name, that was a subject for discussion. Ronnie came up with Cemetery Rovers, guaranteed in his opinion to petrify the opposition. Spencer said Rood End Rovers. I wanted something with Albion in it.

'How about "Odds and Sods"?' said Joey, Mr

Cork's usual name for us. 'Odds and Sods United.'

'You can't have "Sods",' said Trevor. 'They'd not allow it.'

'How about something with Albert Park in it?' said Graham. 'Or Tugg Street?' where he lived.

By and by, but only because we had to get the form filled in, we settled on Malt Shovel Rovers. There'd be no other team with a pub in it, we reckoned. Not for the under-twelves.

In the afternoon we continued our search for players. We needed a goalkeeper, an unsought-after position for most boys. You'd get fifteen centre forwards on the bottom pitch with hardly a goalie in sight. Billy Shakespeare was proposed – 'Shakespeare in goal!' – but proved unavailable. Snapped up already by the Cubs.

Then Spencer had a brainwave. There was a man named Ice Cream Jack. He kept a shop – Capinelli's – at the top of Tugg Street which sold loads of stuff, including his own home-made ice cream. He also travelled the streets in his horse and cart selling cornets, wafers and such from a milk churn. Anyway, Ice Cream Jack had a son, another Tommy as it happened. He was big and slow-witted, never went to school; never talked much either. Now and then he'd wander into the park and join in a game, if he felt like it. And *he* was a goalie; sort of.

'He's too old,' said Graham.

'No, he's not. He's younger than you. I heard Mrs Milward telling somebody.'

'He's too big,' said Joey.

'Yeah, and Tommy Pye's too little.'

'Add 'em up and divide by two,' suggested Spencer. 'Take the average.'

'That's fair,' said Ronnie.

'Pickin' a team by weight!'

'He'd fill the goal, though,' Graham said.

So on we went through the day, knocking on doors, bumping into boys in the street, rushing off home to do jobs for our mums, charging out again with biscuits, bread and jam and stuff. Feverish, intense, *scalded* really, with life. Up for it. Getting a team up.

Here's a thing that may surprise you. The players that we already had, not to mention those we still had hopes of getting, were good. Some of them, me for instance, were potentially brilliant. Give me a ball and try and get it back. I was like a slippery eel. The ball stuck to my foot like glue. We owed it all, I realize now, to Mr Cork and the bottom pitch. The boys on the bottom pitch, a great soup of boys, a swamp of them . . . played football. In September when we started none of us were much good. Otherwise we'd have made it to the top pitch. But six months later, by Easter, it was a different story. Evolution it was: the survival of the fittest. If only Darwin could have seen us, he'd have worked his theory out a whole lot sooner. To get hold of the ball, even for an instant, to get a kick even, you needed determination. To hang on to it, dribble with it, *score* . . . well.

Sunday was a wasteland. Everywhere shut up. Sunday school (they had a team up) in the morning. A visit – three buses! – to Great-Aunt Phoebe's over Brierley Hill in the afternoon. A cup of her lethal tea, brewed so long it was like liquorice. A trip to Brierley Hill cemetery. Flowers on Mabel's grave. The squealing of the pigs in Marsh & Baxter's sausage factory. A clip round the ear from Mum for something or other. Home on the buses. Bed.

By Monday morning back at school we had ten players, including Tommy Ice Cream, Tommy Pye and both the Prossers. We got our final player at playtime: Arthur Toomey. There's something else here I should explain. All those boys, you'd think we'd be spoilt for choice. But it had also to do with *where you lived*, which streets you lived in: territory.

It wasn't laid down, there were no boundaries marked. Only some sort of early knowledge that kids, boys especially, acquired, not long after they could walk and toddle off somewhere.

Arthur Toomey was, I suppose you'd say, the white sheep of the family: an easygoing, scruffy of course, dirty even, boy who rarely if ever punched other boys or acquired their possessions. He didn't have many friends in the school, but, being a Toomey, no enemies.

There were too many Toomeys, an entire dangerous tribe of them living in a pair of knocked-together (and knocked-about) council semis behind the Malt Shovel. An intimidating, lawless crew who settled their quarrel with the world collectively with clenched fists.

Where we lived in those days, the people were poor, all of them, all the time. Even so there were degrees of poverty. Think of all the shades of green, say, in a paint shop. The Sorrells, Spencer's family, were respectable. Mr Sorrell wore a jacket with a collar and tie and worked in a wages office. We were poorer but respectable too. The insurance man called once a week. We saved regularly in two clubs for bedding, clothes and Christmas. The unrespectable poor, the Skidmores for example, spent too much time in pubs and too much money on the dogs. As for the Toomeys, Mr Toomey mostly did not wear a *shirt.* Their garden resembled a bomb site. On the only occasion I entered their house, there was a newspaper on the table for a cloth and jam-jar cups.

At dinnertime – bulging with meat and potato pie, carrots and gravy, little squares of bread, semolina and jam – we had our first team meeting. Games of tick'n'release, horses and riders, marbles, buttons and the like were going on all around us. Amos was up to his usual tricks in the toilets. Mrs Harris was on duty.

We talked about team selection, training and the money Spencer and I were owed.

'A tanner each, I make it,' I said. 'Ice Cream Tommy won't pay.'

'He should, though,' said Trevor. 'His dad's got loads.'

'What about me?' said Tommy Pye. 'I'm only seven.'

'Ask your mummy,' said Joey, laughing. 'Give her a cuddle.'

Then Wyatt joined in. He was eager to tell us how he had had a bath last night and trimmed his toenails. Wyatt was one of our later acquisitions. A tall, thin boy, with ears set sharply at right angles to his head. He looked like a wing nut. He was a good player all the same, good-natured and with a touching belief – fostered no doubt by his loving mother, grandmother and four sisters – in the intrinsic interest of his entire life to everybody he ever met.

Presently, as though on a prearranged signal, Mr Reynolds and Mr Cork came striding down the steps, across the playground and into the toilets. They hauled Amos and two or three others out of there and marched them off.

The bell rang and we all lined up in our classes. As he departed to join his line of first-year tiddlers, Tommy Pye tugged Spencer's sleeve.

'The shirts,' he said, in his little piping voice, ''ave they got numbers on 'em?'

5
Edna May Prosser Arrives

The match was played till after dark
Till gates were closed on Albert Park
By shadowy boys whose shapes dissolved
Into the earth as it revolved.

Friendly Matches (2001)

The shirts. The shirts! I blame that application form. No mention of shirts there, team colours or anything. Of course, they were expecting school teams mostly, teams already kitted out. It was a cock-up in the Parks and Cemeteries department. This competition, this cup, was a bit of a rush job. Somebody'd had a bright idea and not followed it through. All the same, there we were, an established *named* team, with melodramas of suspense and triumph blossoming in our heads, commentaries already in rehearsal, whispered aloud in the privacy of lavatories and bathrooms. 'It's Wyatt now, the ball glued to his foot . . .' And no shirts.

Spencer, Ronnie, Arthur Toomey and I sat in the sheds again – more rain – and contemplated our situation. Ways of obtaining the shirts were proposed.

'We could get our mums to make 'em!' Spencer.

'Each of us get a shirt and dye 'em!' Me.

'Nick 'em.' Ronnie.

Meanwhile, Arthur was digging away with his penknife into the scarred boards of the shed without speaking. He was listening, though.

Spencer had a bag of chips and batters which he was passing round, cautiously. He'd cover the bag with his free hand, allowing you just room enough to secure a single chip or batter. Archie, the Purnells' lop-sided dog, lop-sidled up. He could smell a chip a mile off. Joey Skidmore arrived. So could he.

Other members of the team appeared, some non-members too. It was early evening and Tommy Pye was there. No Tommy Ice Cream yet. The rain had eased. Coat goals were set up and a game began. Spencer stayed out of things, attending to his few remaining chips. Archie, unable to choose between the ball and food, darted irresolutely back and forth. In between the surges of the game – the ball in the pond for a while – in the street! – we kicked around this business with the shirts. The best we came up with, Joey's idea, was just to turn up anyway and expect to play.

By and by the first of the mothers arrived, Mrs Pye. She removed her tiny son from the pitch. To compensate and console him, and shut him up, she stuck a lolly in his mouth. Tommy Pye, the prodigy with a ball, deceiver of boys twice his size, destined for fame in years to come with Aston Villa, departed holding his mummy's hand. Mrs Glue was next. She said not a word but stood with her hands on her hips till Graham reluctantly acknowledged her existence. And he departed.

No other mothers appeared that evening, though their influence was felt. Trevor left, off to the hospital again. Edna May Prosser arrived with a message for her brothers from *their* mother: Come. Home. Now. Edna May, a bold girl with a liking, it was commonly supposed, for Joey Skidmore, joined in the game, dispossessing her brother (Malcolm? Patrick?) and charging off down the wing with the ball. She hit a decent cross into the middle which Joey himself, as it happened, bundled in.

Tommy Ice Cream arrived in his usual ankle-length coat, worn in all weathers. He ambled on to the pitch, shrugged off the coat and revealed one brand-new bright green goalie's jersey. He made no comment, wearing also his usual expressionless expression, but occupied the nearest goal. He had new boots too, his trousers tucked in his socks. In the distance, Ice Cream Jack himself in *his* long coat could be seen hovering near the gates, checking out Tommy's reception. Was his horse and cart outside, I wondered? Was his ice cream?

At seven o'clock the park bell rang. Mr Phipps rode up on his bicycle inviting us, in his amiable way, to clear off out of it. Out in the streets darkness was falling, gathering around the yellow street lights. The air was smoky and damp, old man Cutler's latest still smouldering defiantly after the rain. He himself was off to the pub. Street lights, like everything else, were different in those days. Less light, but more colour. Bottle-green privet hedges, rosy-red house bricks and garden walls, the fading purpling sky itself. Spencer and I went home, Tommy Ice Cream accompanying us part of the way. Well, sort of. He was with us in his fashion, that is, silent and two paces to the rear. If you spoke to him, he pulled his head down deeper into his coat. If you waited for him to catch up, he waited for you to keep going.

At the corner of Seymour Road he went his own way. Spencer was telling me a tale that Wyatt had told him. Not about haircuts or toenails, but a body. A dead body, Wyatt claimed, had been found in the toilets up in the cemetery. It was all muddied up (like us!) but wearing a suit. We speculated about this body. Was it a murder? Had somebody just gone in there and died? Had some *body* been dug up? I suggested we walk up Cemetery Road, which conveniently divided the cemetery in two, and see what we could see, a police car perhaps. Spencer was enthusiastic at first, but it was pretty well night now and both of us thought better of it. A dog chased a hissing cat right out in front of us, which made us jump. Edna May came bowling along on her bike – no lights – looking for Joey maybe. I felt low, miserable really, thinking about those non-existent shirts. Outside Starkey's in the glow from the window I spotted a Turf packet on the pavement. It was fairly dry, protected under the awning. Turf cigarettes had pictures of footballers in them, fifty in the set. Not cigarette cards exactly, not separate, but part of the packet itself. (My dad preferred Woodbines, though he'd smoke Turf sometimes at my request.) I snatched the packet up. It was a player I already had, but useful for swaps. I felt a sudden surge of joy.

A few days later, early on a Monday morning, Spencer lifted the latch of their back veranda gate, which opened on to an entry, and fell over a large object. It was a parcel: brown paper, roughly wrapped and held together with string. No name. No address. No stamps. There were dirty hand prints on the outside and what looked like tea stains (or, Ronnie reckoned, blood). But inside, crisp and new and folded beautifully, as Spencer found, inside there was a set of shirts.

6

Spencer Sorrell and Ronnie Horsfield

'That's a nice tin of beans, I'll have that.'
Burglar Bill (1977)

Cat on a Wall. Spencer Sorrell was my best true friend, not that I would ever have told *him*. We had known each other about a year. He was a medium sort of boy, dark hair combed flat to his head with a knife-like parting. He sometimes wore two pairs of socks to make his legs look thicker. He had a mild, hesitant expression and smelled of furniture polish. (Everything in Spencer's house gleamed from his mother's relentless attentions.) Yes, a true friend. I remember when I was ill in bed one time and he came round with a present. He left it on the step; my mother scared him, she scared most people. It was a tomato, picked from his own plant, with a little face stuck on it.

Spencer was tactful. Early on in our friendship he witnessed at close range one of Mum's mad explosions with me sent flying across the yard, and made no comment, nor did he subsequently pry. Despite the sunray treatment he regularly received, his face was pale. He had spent some months away in Malvern at an open-air school or sanatorium. There was, my mother informed me, 'a patch on his lung'.

Actually, most faces in Oldbury were pale then, or dirty at best. Sunlight struggled to penetrate the town's protective shield. Spencer attended his sunray clinic on Tuesday mornings. After a time and a bit of badgering, he told me about it. He had to wear blue goggles and sit in a circle with other children around this special lamp, a dazzling column of light. Most of the others were younger than him; all of them, him included, were just in their underpants or knickers. Now and then they joined hands and moved around.

Spencer revealed all this, wished he hadn't and swore me to secrecy.

'Don't tell!'

'I won't. Do you sing songs in that circle?'

'On y'mother's grave.'

'Do you dance?'

'Promise.'

The love of Spencer's life was his cat. He came home from school for his dinner on certain days, mainly, in my opinion, to play with her. Her name was Minnie and *she* was older than him. She would roll on the floor to have her tummy tickled. In her youth, Spencer recalled, she would leap like a goalkeeper to catch a ball of silver paper tossed in her direction. In old age she was more sedate. Spencer called her 'Mrs Furbag'.

I learnt much about cats from Spencer. We'd had a cat in Stone Street. Watching Spencer with his, I felt ashamed of what I'd done with ours, rolling it up in the bedclothes, terrorizing and then *forgiving* it. When we moved, it ran off. Who can blame it?

Spencer's dad was as soft as he was. Sometimes when Minnie was up on their high wall, he and Spencer joined forces to bring her in. Mr Sorrell would bend down below the wall, Spencer would pat his back and call to the cat. Sometimes he'd position a cushion to protect the cat's paws from his father's bony spine. And down she'd jump.

The Frankenstein of Frogs. Ronnie Horsfield was a friend too, but more recent, harder. He had attached himself to us in the last few months. Ronnie was small and wiry and often wore a balaclava. He smelled – pleasantly, in my opinion

– of dogs. Two slept in his room. He lived with his gran; his parents were never mentioned.

There was a huge hand-painted message, I remember, on the end wall of Ronnie's house:

WELCOME HOME GEORGE

with a roughly painted Union Jack above it, and the date: 14 August 1946. So who was George? Ronnie's dad, perhaps, coming home from the war? The message and the flag were fading year by year. But if he was welcomed home, this George, where was he now?

What Ronnie was good at was climbing: walls, gates, drainpipes, anything. In the park behind the boathouse there was a pair of trees where it was possible, with some daring and skill, to climb up the one and down the other. Ronnie and I were among the elite who could accomplish this. Yes, Ronnie might look like a sparrow, but his strength/weight ratio was off the scale. He could swing across between those trees one-handed like a chimp.

But, when all was said and done, the thing about Ronnie Horsfield was, he had *a reputation*. There were stories and rumours about him. He had no great talent apart from climbing, was not particularly clever or brave, and yet he seemed quite effortlessly to get his own way. Nobody ever bothered him, not even Amos. His reputation was both mysterious and horrible: things he was *supposed to have done*. He had a level gaze. Even Mr Cork thought twice before banging Ronnie Horsfield's desk.

It's all about perspective and scale. To the adults, except Mrs Milward maybe, we were little boys. *Amos* was a little boy. But in the playground, or anywhere with his fists up, Amos was a colossus, a terror, the biggest shark in the sea. And Ronnie too: a skinny scrap, a shrimp of a boy, but in our minds at times, if the truth were told, a regular Dr Frankenstein no less. Of frogs.

A Sad Jelly. My friends, you'll note, were somewhat odd; I was the normal one. I did a bad thing once, it's true, and more than once. ('That's a nice pencil sharpener, I'll have that.') Took Dennis Johnson's marbles too, burgled his desk one wet playtime, I'm ashamed to say. Sorry, Dennis. Also, I had this talent for making things up. If Spencer taught me cats, I taught him alibis. One time we were fooling around with some matches and he got a burn hole through two thicknesses of sock. He was greatly agitated. What could he tell his mother?

'Tell her . . . tell her you fell on a lighted cigarette!' A convincing explanation, I thought. It had worked with my mother.

There again, what's normal anyway? What's odd? That whole town was populated with oddities, as I remember it, broken and damaged people that the doctors had not yet tidied up or locked away. Men with missing arms, dogs with missing legs. Ice Cream Jack had a great black built-up boot on one of his feet. A boy in our class was covered top to toe with livid flaky scabs. Bobby Edwards ran errands for his sister to the shops with a note of what to get, creases of concentration on his face. And he was forty-six. Mrs Moore shook permanently like a sad jelly. Likewise, mysteries and unlikelihoods abounded. Mr Reynolds always offered you a sweet – a Fisherman's Friend or pear drop – after whacking you with his cane. There was a ghost in the boathouse, a body in the cemetery toilets, a parcel of football shirts conjured up from nowhere on Spencer Sorrell's step.

7

The Boy Who Looked Like a Yacht

THE OLDBURY AND DISTRICT
QUEEN ELIZABETH II CORONATION CUP

ROUND 1: MALT SHOVEL ROVERS V.
TIVIDALE PRIMARY 'B'

VENUE: BARNFORD PARK DATE: 4 APRIL 1953

KICK-OFF: 10.30 A.M.

The Team

Goalkeeper	Thomas Capanelli
Right back	Malcolm Prosser
Left back	Patrick Prosser
Right half	Graham Glue
Centre half	Joey Skidmore
Left half	Arthur Toomey
Outside right	Trevor Darby
Inside right	Me
Centre forward	Ronnie Horsfield
Inside left	Tommy Pye
Outside left	Wyatt
Manager	Mr S. Sorrell

We sat in the changing rooms, a painted wooden shed with splintery benches and coat hooks fixed to the walls. Bars of weak sunlight filtered through the dirty windows, dust danced in the air. Spencer and I distributed the shirts. Tommy Pye was delighted with his, though miles too big and having no number. The others were less pleased, mainly on account of the colours.

'What's this? Pink, is it? Purple?'

'It's lilac, actually,' said Spencer.

'Lilac?' Joey Skidmore was almost spitting with disgust. '*Lilac?* We'll look like a –'

'Lilac like a,' said Ronnie.

'Look like a, like a load of . . . bunch of . . .'

'Prats?' said Wyatt.

'Prats,' said Joey.

Meanwhile, little Tommy had disappeared into his shirt as though it were a tent.

'You told us they were Albion colours [blue and white stripes],' said Graham.

The Parks and Cemeteries man stuck his head round the door.

'Five minutes, boys,' he said.

'They were,' said Spencer placidly. 'There was an accident.'

A face, Edna May's, smiled briefly in at a window,

prompting a couple of trouserless boys to scuttle out of sight.

'In the wash house,' Spencer said.

Trevor was twirling around now, holding his shirt out like a dance frock.

'Accident?' cried Joey. 'It's a bloody pantomime!'

The moaning continued but was eventually overtaken by the sense of occasion we all felt. To step out there, lilac shirts or not, into that watery morning light, on to that proper pitch with its fresh white lines, goalposts, nets! The grass, in truth, could have done with a trim – send for Mr Cotterill – but the excitement, the peculiar mixture of shyness and showing off; I could hardly think straight.

The game kicked off. Ten minutes later we were 3–0 down. A wild rush by their entire team into our penalty area produced the first, and, building cleverly on this success, the second likewise. The third goal involved the Prosser twins and a high corner. Both of them went for it. Unluckily, Malcolm, who could head a ball, was beaten to it by Patrick, who couldn't. It skimmed the top of his head and flew into the goal.

The crowd was going wild, all twenty of them.

Edna May was there with a friend. Mrs Glue. My mum, frowning as ever, with Dinah tugging at her lead. Albert and Rufus Toomey arrived late and were lounging now behind the Tividale goal, blowing smoke from their cigarettes towards the goalie. A cluster of Tividale supporters waving scarves and such stood at the halfway line.

Now it was our turn. First goal, a wild rush by all of us into *their* penalty area; second, an almost intentional back-heel from Ronnie, and the third, a prodigious dribble from Tommy Pye. Tommy Pye was the instant darling of the crowd, even as he ran on to the pitch. The mothers, Tividale's included, 'Ooe'd' and 'Ah'd' whenever he touched the ball and protested loudly if he was tackled. Anyway, Tommy picked up a rebound – the ball in games like this spent half its life ricocheting around – and headed for the goal. In that billowing shirt of his he looked like a small yacht. On he went, left foot, right foot, dropping his shoulder, feinting this way and that – oh yes, he had it all. None of the Tividale kids could stop him, nor could he stop himself, but ended up in the back of the net, ball, goalie and all.

The game continued with more goals in the second half and some heroics from Tommy Ice Cream. He really was a big boy for his age. He didn't move around much, but stuck out his arms and legs and the ball often as not just hit him. He was impervious to pain and had a goal kick like a siege gun.

With only minutes remaining, the score was 7–all. Tommy Ice Cream had blocked a shot with his knees. Advancing through the horde of Tividale centre forwards, he prepared to explode a kick upfield. At that moment I was out on the touchline tying a bootlace. I called for the ball. Tommy, surprisingly alert and willing, threw it to me. I embarked on a dribble of my own. With most of the opposition behind me, I approached the halfway line, beat one tackle, beat another, resisted a shove in the back from a muscly little boy and lifted my gaze towards the goal. Wyatt then came steaming up on my left. Hardly knowing what I did, I drifted right, took the defender with me and *passed the ball* to Wyatt. The surprise, to me, of this action caused me to stop stone dead. I watched as Wyatt, in his bony angular fashion, galloped on towards the goal and with a carefree swing of his leg hammered the ball high across the Tividale goalie's outstretched arms, hands, fingers – and into the net.

It was a transforming moment. On top of all the predictable feelings, those I shared with the others – exhilaration, joy – there was this extra, mysterious, still-to-be-worked-out pleasure. I had *made* a goal. Yes – and it was the winner.

8

Receivers of Stolen Goods

The walk home from Barnford Park, down that ordinary hill, past those nothing-in-particular houses, gates and gardens, those matter-of-fact post boxes, phone boxes, telegraph poles, privet hedges, sweet wrappers, chip papers, fag ends, matchsticks, all the endless paraphernalia of life . . . was magical. We talked in one great tangled skein or snowball of words that rolled on down the hill with us inside it, while our faces glowed with the other, the inexpressible, wordless stuff.

JOEY That was never a penalty! (*Joey had upended their centre forward and the divot of turf he was stood on.*)

GRAHAM Right!

RONNIE Did y'see that back-heel?

WYATT Did y'see . . . (*Wyatt forgets what he intended to say.*)

TOMMY PYE Their lot had oranges. We should have oranges.

RONNIE Ask 'Mr Sorrell' then.

ARTHUR I can get oranges.

GRAHAM Did y'see –

PATRICK I'm better as a forward really. I don't like it at left back.

JOEY Well y'scored (*that 'skid-off-his-head' own goal*) anyway.

MALCOLM *I* don't like it at right back.

TREVOR Look, Joey, here's Edna May. You love her.

JOEY No, I don't.

TREVOR You said –

JOEY No, I never!

SPENCER We should let Tommy Ice Cream take the free kicks, y'know.

RONNIE Yeah – he'd blast 'em.

JOEY Smash 'em!

RONNIE Annihilate 'em!

JOEY Tommy, Tommy! (*Attempts to give Tommy Ice Cream, two paces to the rear, a hug. Tommy falls back still further and retreats into his coat.*)

EDNA MAY (*At the kerb on her bike.*) Who y'playin' next?

JOEY Who wants to know?

TREVOR Joey says he loves you.

JOEY No, I never.

BRENDA (*Bissell, Edna May's friend.*) She loves him.

EDNA MAY *You* love him.

TREVOR 'E loves 'er.

(Exit, laughing, Brenda and Edna May.)

ME Did y'see me lay that one on a plate?
WYATT Did y'see . . . (*And forgets again.*)
SPENCER You should tie your laces up more often –
JOEY It was never a penalty, though.
SPENCER – there's space on the wings.

Mrs Sorrell and the Shirts. It occurs to me I have yet to explain the business with the shirts. Well, that 'accident' Spencer spoke of happened like this: Mrs Sorrell washed them. It was a *Monday*, you see, when the shirts were discovered and Monday was washday. Mrs Sorrell was not concerned with where the shirts had come from – Spencer implied that I had something to do with it – but very concerned about *where they might have been*, nicely folded or not. Spencer couldn't possibly wear (or even handle) something that she herself had not rubbed with soap, pummelled and scrubbed, boiled in the copper, wrung out in the mangle and ironed to perfection. Washday was an institution in that town. Mothers competed to get their sheets and such out flapping on the lines in communal yards or adjacent gardens. Wash houses clattered and rang with their industry. Steam billowed from open windows, smoke rose from chimneys. Never mind football competitions for the kids, how about a

Coronation Washday Cup for the mothers? Mrs Sorrell would have made the final; you could've bet on my mum too.

So the shirts were washed. Unfortunately, other stuff found its way into the boiler as well, including a pair of Angela's school socks (Spencer's sister). Holly Lodge colours: purple and green. Brand new.

The shirts were also brand new. Interestingly, the maker's labels had been removed. Where they had come from perplexed us all. Later that same morning on the way to school, Spencer and I met up with Ronnie and Graham Glue. The news was circulated and explanations sought.

'It's somebody trying to help us,' said Graham. 'A secret supporter.'

'Why leave 'em on Spencer's step?' said I.

'He's the manager,' said Ronnie.

'Got his name on the form,' Graham said.

'Why cut the labels out?' said I.

'Are you sure there was no writing on the parcel – no stamps?' said Graham.

'Nothing,' Spencer said. 'It was never posted.'

'Somebody –'

'Secret supporter,' said Graham.

'Somebody,' said I, 'crept down your entry in the dead of night and –'

'Why cut the labels out?' said Ronnie and answered it himself. 'Nicked.'

The possibility of a shy or secretive benefactor appealed to us.

'Ice Cream Jack!' cried Joey, who had joined the walkers. ''E's got money.'

'Yeah, new jersey for Tommy, new shirts for us,' said Graham.

'Why not just hand 'em over?' said I. 'Why cut the labels out?'

The possibility that we were the receivers of stolen goods also appealed. Stealing was by no means the worst of crimes in our eyes in those days. Scrumped rock-hard pears from the vicarage, peas in the pod from the allotments, bits and pieces from Milward's, other kids' marbles. Not all of us did all of it, but most of us did some of it, and none of us, except Spencer maybe, wholly disapproved. Of course, the advantage of *dyed* stolen goods was plain to everybody. The cops, if they were on the trail at all, would be looking for Albion kit not French night-shirts, as Joey described them.

Just then we encountered Albert and Rufus Toomey. They were squashed into a phone box and up to no good. Rufus rapped on the glass; Arthur was with us now, eating his breakfast: cold toast. He waved to his brothers. Albert pressed his reddish face to the glass. If you didn't know him better, you might well have suspected him . . . of smiling.

Anyway, after the match – our Tividale triumph – and the long walk home down Barnford Hill, there were jobs to do. Helping Mum to make the beds, running errands: bone meal for the hens, dog biscuits for Dinah. I remember those biscuits, bone-shaped some of them, all different colours and sold loose from a barrel. I enjoyed them almost as much as Dinah did, especially the black ones. They were good for my teeth, apparently, and gave me a glossy coat.

I had money to earn too, errands and such to run for Mrs Moore. Mrs Moore was our nearest neighbour, and the first to make us welcome when we moved up from Stone Street. She suffered from a kind of palsy and shook all over. Bravely, in these circumstances, she arrived at our house amid the boxes and piles of furniture with a tray, biscuits and a pot of tea. Mrs Moore was a gentle, trusting soul. She promoted in me a degree of good manners that would have surprised my parents and astounded the school.

In contrast, my mother was explosive. I got

clouted a couple of times while making the beds, accused of eating Dinah's biscuits – indignantly denied – another clout. At teatime my invisible dad showed up, witnessed the hurling of a failed pie out through the kitchen window into the yard, and departed. He took refuge on his allotment. I retreated to the park with Dinah, and later still in the gathering gloom to the lavatory. By torchlight I harassed in my turn an unoffending spider and read the paper. There was a small rectangular window through which the rising moon was visible. I gazed at the square of newsprint in my hand, but hardly saw it. My thoughts were somewhere else. 'It's Ahlberg now, the ball glued to his foot . . .'

9

The Stanley Matthews Football Book

On Monday morning in assembly Mr Reynolds talked to the whole school about boys playing on bomb sites, boys trespassing in Messrs Danks's factory yard and storage areas, nits, Jesus and the Coronation Cup.

A boy named Horace Crumpton had fallen and dislocated his shoulder while fooling around in a derelict house. Mr Reynolds felt sure we could learn a lesson from him. Horace took a bow, embarrassed and pleased with himself, arm in a sling. Other boys, so far unidentified, had been chased out of Danks's on Saturday night by the watchman. It was Amos and his lot treading the boilers again, but Mr Reynolds was not to know this. He was sick and tired of getting phone calls to his home, he said, and promised retribution.

On a happier note, Mr Reynolds invited us to bask in the achievements of both our teams in the

Coronation Cup. They had done tremendously well. The 'B' team had lost narrowly to Rolfe Street, while the 'A' team had simply slaughtered the Good Shepherd, 14–3. Three cheers were called for and supplied. No mention of us. Mr Reynolds, Mr Cork and the others had yet to hear of *our* achievements, though by the end of the day word had spread. Mr Cork, it was reported, took offence. He hammered a few more desks than usual, including his own. He saw it as a comment on the lawless times in which we now lived. If Rood End had needed three teams, or been capable of them, he was the one to say so, not Master Joseph bloomin' Skidmore or Mr Spencer blinkin' Sorrell.

By Wednesday Mr Cork had simmered down (as far as he was likely to). At 1.30 p.m. sixty-six boys trooped out of the school, Amos and Vincent Loveridge leading the way, Mr Cork to the rear. A low and heavy pancake of smog overhung the town. There was no wind. The air was pungent, full of sulphur, soot and worse. The smoke from old man Cutler's bonfire rose straight up in a white column, adding its contribution, with a smaller offering of bluer smoke from old man Cutler's pipe.

We arrived at GKN's sports ground. Mr Cork – proudly? stubbornly? – saw no reason to alter his arrangements. The 'A' team played the 'B' team on the top pitch, the odds and sods were left to their own devices on the bottom. And yet I wonder now, wasn't he the least bit curious? Did he not take a peep, perhaps, now and then? Notice the odd – sod – flash of skill?

The bottom pitch was not stuck in its ways. Instead of two teams and one match, we sorted ourselves into four teams and two matches. There was plenty of room, if you didn't mind long grass and the occasional heavy roller. Spencer had provided himself with a whistle. The first time he blew it, Mr Cork came thundering down the bank and grabbed it off him. Two whistles! It was a recipe for anarchy.

Spencer, as you will have gathered, was no footballer himself. He'd make up the numbers, if required, otherwise his preferred position was outside outside left. But Spencer had an enquiring mind, took things seriously. If he was the manager he was going to manage.

Spencer had two books in his possession: a small cash book from his dad's office in which he made tactical notes (and kept account of who still owed us money), and *The Stanley Matthews Football Book.* I can picture this book even now. I especially delighted in the sequences of little photographs showing Stanley Matthews and his Blackpool team-mate Stanley Mortensen. They demonstrated Matthews's amazing dribbling skills. Spencer was more interested in moves and positional play, the 'ball inside the full back' (except with us there never was a full back), the 'wall pass' and so on. His two big ideas, the means by which we were to triumph over St Saviour's, our next opponents, were (1) that we should pass the ball, and (2) that we should stick to our positions. Team sheets, you see, while they might look official, were pure fiction. Right back, left back, it didn't mean a thing. The Prosser brothers complained about their positions, disliked being *labelled* as full backs, but never allowed it to restrict their movements. The main thing was, attackers were attackers, and defenders were attackers. It was an attacking game. On the other hand, an even greater influence was the ball. The ball was a magnet; where it went we went. So in a way we were all defenders . . . on occasion.

We had got most of our team together playing Tony Leatherland's lot. Both the Tommys were missing, of course, and Trevor Darby. His gran had finally died; it was her funeral that afternoon. Spencer's influence on the game was not great. He refereed, attempting valiantly to be impartial and persuade the players of anything at all. He urged us to pass, run into space, hold our positions. Meanwhile, the fog was thickening. Up on the top pitch the wraith-like figure of Mr Cork flitted here and there, yelling, waving his arm, blasting his whistle. His influence was not great either.

Suddenly, from nowhere, out of the sulphurous air, Tommy Ice Cream emerged, removed his coat and occupied our goal. He ignored the resident goalie, who gratefully trotted off to take up a more attacking position. Some of the kids gave Tommy sidelong looks. He both fascinated and scared them. He was, or seemed anyway, dangerously unpredictable. If he got the ball in his grasp, they wondered, would he ever let it go? His dark eyebrows met menacingly in the middle of his face. He didn't look like he could take a joke.

Eventually, the atmosphere became too impenetrable, too pungent even for Mr Cork. He called it a day, and it was only three o'clock. The office building which overlooked the sports ground shone like a lighthouse. Out on the Birmingham Road, buses, bikes and cars sailed by in ghostly fashion.

Ronnie, Spencer and I were huddled together outside Milward's. Ronnie was reading aloud from the paper, the five-line, three-sentence match report on our game with Tividale. My defence-splitting pass, I grieved to hear, got no mention. Mr and Mrs Smith appeared out of the fog, caught briefly in the haze of light from Milward's window. They had a pram with a baby in it. Mrs Smith greeted me. I felt myself begin to blush and could not look at her. Earlier in the week, despite all protests on my behalf, my mum had dragged me round to see Mrs Smith lying upstairs in her bed with the baby wrapped in a blanket beside her. I was much embarrassed by the whole business. I knew more or less how babies were made. What I couldn't understand was how Mr and Mrs Smith could bear to walk the streets with the baby, where everybody could see them and know what it was they had been up to.

The Smiths were swallowed up in the gloom. Mrs Milward rapped sharply on the window and shooed us away. Archie trotted up, sniffed around, trotted off. A huge black car came slowly, silently into view. Solemn men in black suits were visible through the windows. Headlights lit up but did not penetrate the solid air. And there, pale and frowning, like a little lord almost in his unfamiliar suit and collar and tie, was Trevor. The car, and the second car behind it, moved on and disappeared. Trevor in a car, I thought. The first time in his life, perhaps. (It was!) Mrs Milward knocked once more on the glass. A kid on roller skates whizzed by. And we went home.

10

Treading the Boilers

Football boots in those days were massive objects. It's a wonder to me how our little spindly legs could raise them off the ground, let alone kick anything. The shape of the boot was *boot*-shaped, not carpet slipper-shaped as it is now. They had rock-hard toe caps, and studs were hammered into their soles like a blacksmith shoeing a horse. (Play football in them? You could have marched out of Russia in them.) To soften this rigid, clog-like footwear you needed dubbin, a kind of brown grease, used also on footballs.

Footballs in those days were like dumb-bells without the bar in between, or those stone balls you sometimes saw on the top of posh gateways. I have seen boys head a ball and fall backwards into a sitting position, stunned. When a ball was wet it was like a concrete sponge. When it was dry and well dubbined it would skid off your head –

remember Prosser's own goal? – like a baby on a slide.

And then there was the lace. A football consisted of a stitched leather outside with an inflatable rubber inside. Once you'd blown a ball up, you had to lace it up, a tricky business in itself. No matter how well you did it, the lace stuck out. If you headed the lace, it hurt. The courage – foolhardiness? – of some boys was amazing. They'd head it, it would hurt, and they'd head it again. Footballs made more of an impression on boys' heads back then than teachers, or Mr Cotterill even.

It was Thursday evening. A gang of us were sitting out in Joey Skidmore's yard, admiring a litter of puppies and discussing the forthcoming game. The Skidmores' yard was like an outpost of Dudley Zoo: cats and dogs, hens, chickens, a couple of ducks and God knows how many rabbits. Pigeons too, in their own special loft fixed high up on the end wall which was actually the property of the Creda. At other times, in season, you could find tin baths full of fish or frogs, linnets even (caught by Mr Skidmore), suspended in their home-made wooden cages from hooks along the sunlit wash-house wall, singing away. Recently, I happened upon a rent book from those days in a box of my mother's things. Listed on the back among the 'Conditions of Tenancy' I read this:

5. THE TENANT SHALL NOT

(a) Erect any sheds or structures of any kind without the proper written consent of the Landlord.

(b) Keep poultry or pigeons on the premises unless consent has previously been obtained.

(c) Keep pigs on the premises under any conditions.

I suspect this rent book was written with the Skidmores in mind. They'd kept a pig too, by the way. But that was in the war.

Spencer had some coloured chalks, acquired by me and Trevor from Miss Palmer's chalk box. He had drawn the outline of a pitch on the flagstones and was demonstrating moves.

'See. If you all chase the ball, when you get it there's nobody to pass to.'

'So?' said Wyatt.

'But if *you* –' Spencer drew a little stick-man Wyatt on the left wing – 'stop out there –'

'Like y'did for that goal,' said Arthur.

'And *somebody*,' said I, 'passes to you.'

'You get a clear run,' Spencer said.

'And score,' said Wyatt.

Tommy Pye was present but silent, absorbed in petting one of the puppies. I picked up one myself, its eyes tightly shut, twitching paws, bulging belly smooth as an egg.

Tommy said, 'How much?'

'For one of these?' Joey held his puppy high in the air and kissed its nose. 'It's a pedigree, y'know. Pure boxer spaniel.'

'How much?' said Tommy.

'Well . . . a fiver,' said Joey.

'Five quid!' cried Wyatt and me and Tommy together.

'All right, five bob, then.'

'I ain't got five bob.'

'Ask your mummy,' Joey said. 'Ask y'daddy. Ask y'gran.'

Tommy was silent.

'You can have two for seven-and-six,' said Joey.

A cat sauntered in and sat on Spencer's pitch. A smell of ironing drifted sweetly out from the Skidmores' open kitchen window, the clatter of teacups, Mrs Skidmore singing. Pigeons cooing up in the loft. Late-evening light piling up in the sheltered yard.

'Tell y'what,' said Joey. 'If we win tomorrow, I'll give y'one.'

'Which one?' Tommy's face was a picture.

'The one you're holdin'.'

Silence for a while. Then, 'I love 'im,' Tommy said.

''Er,' said Joey.

Mrs Skidmore stepped out into the yard, pink-faced and stretching her arms above her head. She spotted Spencer's accordion case by the door.

'Hey, Spence – give us a tune!'

Spencer rarely played in public and not that often in private, but had once performed one of his pieces at Mrs Skidmore's request. She was a music lover.

Spencer looked startled. 'Oh, blow it!' He grabbed his accordion, apologized to Mrs Skidmore and bolted across the yard. He had forgotten his lesson again. Soon after, Tommy Pye made his reluctant departure, having previously asked Joey at least half a dozen times if he meant it, if he really meant it, if he really really meant it.

This left me, Joey, Wyatt, Arthur and an ark full of animals. Malcolm Prosser arrived, out of breath, with a bag of chips and bad tidings. Patrick had bust his foot.

'Which one?' said Arthur.

'Left 'un,' Malcolm said.

'So?' said Wyatt, acknowledging that all Patrick ever used his left leg for was standing on.

Patrick, it turned out, had been one of a gang of boys – organized by Amos – who under the cover of fog and darkness had last night revisited Danks's. Treading the boilers involved a dozen or so boys getting inside a boiler and walking in unison, causing it to roll. For some boys, notably Amos, this was an addictive experience. Danks's manufactured boilers of all sizes, used in ships and so on. They stored them in a nearby field. The story goes that the first time boys ever worked this trick, the watchman had a heart attack. There was this huge red-oxided cylinder rolling off all by itself in the moonlight.

Anyway, this time poor old Patrick had got his toes in the way and now had half his leg in plaster. Malcolm was carrying his brother's freshly laundered shirt. The discussion of who should play in Patrick's place began. Spencer would fill in, if we were desperate. Trevor's cousin could be approached or maybe one of the Cubs; they'd been knocked out.

'Bet y'can't play for two teams, though,' said Wyatt.

Trevor himself showed up. He had been off

school since Tuesday, had a black armband sewed to his coat. He seemed all right and, of course, nothing was said.

'I know who we should get,' said Joey.

'Who?'

'Albert Pye.' (Tommy's brother.)

'Albert Pye – he's only five!'

'He's six, actually.'

'Six – he's a infant!'

'Have you seen him play?'

'A baby!'

'Have you *seen* him?'

Wyatt drew a baby in a nappy on the pitch. Sadie, the mother of the pups, ambled lazily out of the house. She flopped down in a sunlit patch and pretty soon the pups had sniffed her out. They snuggled and suckled like a row of little sausages beside her. Mr Skidmore came out and removed his bicycle from the wash house. Mrs Skidmore leant in the doorway with a cup of tea. The sound of Mrs Purnell yelling at Mr Purnell drifted in over the wall. Wyatt was doodling on the pitch. A dog in boots was added to the team. Trevor picked up some chalk and joined in. He drew a little stick-girl with triangular skirt and flying pigtails, and gave Wyatt a nudge.

'*I* know who we should get,' he said.

11

Why Was He Born So Beautiful?

THE OLDBURY AND DISTRICT
QUEEN ELIZABETH II CORONATION CUP

ROUND 2: (QUARTER-FINALS)
ST SAVIOUR'S R.C. PRIMARY V.
MALT SHOVEL ROVERS

VENUE: PERROTT ST. PLAYING FIELD
DATE: 10 APRIL 1953

KICK-OFF: 5.30 P.M.

The Team

Goalkeeper	Thomas Capanelli
Right back	Malcolm Prosser
Left back	Graham Glue
Right half	Trevor Darby
Centre half	Joey Skidmore
Left half	Arthur Toomey
Outside right	Edna May Prosser
Inside right	Me

Centre forward	Ronnie Horsfield
Inside left	Tommy Pye
Outside left	Wyatt
Manager	Mr S. Sorrell

Girls did play football in those days. Not often, but now and then. Not many, but some. Girls did most things, of course: climbed trees, scrumped pears, got into fights. (Never got the cane, though, not from Mr Reynolds anyway.) Alice Bissell, Brenda's cousin, was on probation for shoplifting. Joan Tripp had climbed into Danks's on more than one occasion. And there were others.

Well, we took a vote and between Spencer, 'Baby' Pye and Edna May, Edna May got it. I believe that for some of us the rebellious aspect of this choice appealed. We were a team of outlaws after all. Mr Cork would probably explode, pulverize the entire classroom when he heard. Joey, by the way, was ill at ease. Teased relentlessly by Trevor, he eventually abstained. Spencer voted for Edna May, as did Graham, though he doubted her chances of playing.

'They'll not allow it,' he said.

'They'll allow it,' said Ronnie.

*

The young man from the Parks and Cemeteries department was worried. He was the same young man who had been at the Tividale match. His name was Mr Ash. He'd worried then about Spencer being the manager, and the size and doubtful age of Tommy Ice Cream. Tommy Ice Cream, in his heavy coat, flat cap and with the hint of a moustache, looked about thirty. Technically, Tommy was still a pupil in the school. In earlier times he had sat in Mrs Belcher's backward class, playing with Plasticine and reading or not reading baby books. He had stuck this for a while and then one morning kicked his chair over and walked out. Mrs Belcher tried half-heartedly to detain him. Tommy was big even then. He had a temper and felt no pain. So the school let him go and made no great effort to get him back. Thereafter, Tommy roamed the streets like a gypsy, watched over by his hobbling or horse-drawn dad, and educated himself.

Anyway, this time for Match Number Two Tommy had his birth certificate in an envelope in his pocket. As for Edna May, there she was, shirt, shorts, socks, boots – smiling and bold.

Mr Ash, hardly twenty himself, puffed out his cheeks and thought aloud.

'I'm not so sure about this.'

'About what?' said Ronnie.

'Girls,' said Mr Ash. 'This is a competition for boys . . .'

'It doesn't say so in the rules . . . Sir,' said Spencer. 'Just under-twelves.'

'I'm under twelve,' said Edna May.

'Ah yes . . . the rules,' said Mr Ash.

'I'm under eleven!' Edna May said.

Mr Ash hesitated, opened his mouth to speak, and sighed. He was no match for Spencer and Ronnie, no match for Edna May. To cap it all, reinforcements arrived in the shape of Sister MacPherson. Sister MacPherson was the head of St Saviour's, an impressive bespectacled lady in nun's habit and football boots. She felt Edna May should absolutely play; girls were a match for any boy; wished she'd thought of it. A ball being kicked about came bouncing towards her. Sister MacPherson swivelled and walloped it back with interest. Yes, any boy, she declared; let her play.

There was a real crowd this time, a hundred or so. It was an evening match, so some of the dads were there: shy Mr Sorrell, rowdy Mr Skidmore, glum Mr Glue. Mothers, babies, dogs; riotous kids from both schools. A bunch of girls, friends and foes of Edna May. Monica Copper, it pleased (embarrassed) me to see, was among them. A steady trickle of men from the Perrott Arms with pint mugs in their hands. A policeman on his beat. Ice Cream Jack out in the street, looking in through the railings.

Perrott Street playing field was right in the middle of town. The pitch itself was a beauty, well-grassed and flat with a neat, low, white-painted post and rail running all the way round it, like a picture frame. It enhanced our sense of importance as we finally trotted out. Tommy Pye's shirt fitted him better now, his mum had altered it, but he still looked like Wee Willie Winkie. Joey's shirt looked peculiar. In an effort to subdue its colour, he had gone mad with the bleach. The shirt was paler but worn-out, ancient-looking.

As we lined up for the kick-off, the cry arose from the assembled fathers and other pint-holding experts, 'Get stuck in!' And before even we had kicked anything, 'Get rid of it!' Urged on by Sister MacPherson, St Saviour's pursued the ball into every corner of the pitch. Once again we found ourselves on the losing side, 1–0, 2–0. Spencer's tactics had their drawbacks. Wyatt, with the promise of goal-scoring opportunities, was holding his position on the left wing. Edna May was out on the right. Consequently, in the main mad chase for the ball, we were outnumbered. According to Spencer and Stanley Matthews, positional play was vital. But St Saviour's with their 'tactics' effectively had ten of everything, right backs, left backs, centre forwards. They were everywhere in their hooped old-gold and black shirts, like a swarm of bees.

A lucky rebound got us back in it. A mighty clearance from Tommy Ice Cream bounced awkwardly and caught their goalie a glancing blow on the side of his head. As he spun round looking for the ball – 'It's behind you!' – Tommy Pye arrived, undetected at knee level, and poked it in the net.

Now we were starting to play. Arthur got the ball, passed to Wyatt and, urged on by Spencer, ran beyond their defenders for the return. Wyatt, though, had only undertaken to receive passes, not give them. With Arthur and others creating confusion, and me yelling at Wyatt to pass it – 'Bloody *pass* it!' – he moved serenely inside, took a couple of galloping strides and slammed a goal from twenty-five yards.

It was still 2–all at half-time. Tommy Ice Cream had blocked shots with various parts of his body. He was fairly well covered in mud. (The pitch was lush, low-lying and cut up easily.) Edna May had distinguished herself with some bold tackles and a cross-cum-shot which skimmed the opposition's bar. The crowd was struck by the unusual composition of our side: girls and infants on the pitch and a grown man in goal. The traffic of alcoholic refreshments from the Perrott Arms continued: full pints one way, empty the other. Most of the men were in overalls, their hands and faces grimed and dirty with work, only their mouths washed clean by the beer.

We gathered on the halfway-line in a cluster around Spencer. Mrs Pye was giving her Tommy a clean-up of his own with spit and a hankie. Mr Glue gloomily anticipated defeat unless Graham pulled his socks up. Mr Skidmore urged all of us to get stuck in and stop 'faffin' about'. Wyatt had befriended a passing dog and was busy turning its ears inside out. Rufus and Albert Toomey came forward shyly almost, *conspiratorially*, with a paper sack, buttoned up inside Rufus's coat, of oranges. Albert produced a fearsome-looking knife and cut them up. Tommy Ice Cream ate his bit and, before anyone could stop him, swallowed the peel with it.

The second half was a disjointed affair. Perrott Street playing field was small: one pitch with a path around it, shrubberies and flowerbeds, swings, toilets, and that was it. This did not prevent gangs of kids from (dis)organizing rival games of their own on the touchline and behind the goals. Sometimes we found ourselves with three balls to choose from. Dogs sauntered on to the pitch; a pair of them got into a snarling vicious fight and had to be separated. The referee was gradually losing his temper. He urged the grown-ups to control their kids, and their dogs. But the dads in general were no help, becoming, as they did, increasingly light-hearted and rowdy. They passed loud comments about the match and the referee, who got grumpier still. A short fat man with yellow hair and a penetrating pub voice climbed up on a bench and began singing:

'Why was he born so beautiful?
Why was he born at all!'

Anyway, they scored another but we scored three. The first, a composed, *placed* penalty from me – I had been practising; the last, the best, the most 'faffed about' one of the lot: Joey to Ronnie – Ronnie to Edna May and back to Ronnie (a wall pass!) – down the line to Tommy Pye – square ball to Joey, who had not stopped running – Goal!

A word about celebration. There was less of it then. We'd leap about and yell all right, get a pat on the back maybe, but none of this kissing and cuddling stuff, high-fives and all that. Some of the mothers though . . . Mrs Skidmore, for instance, made an embarrassing fuss of Joey when the final whistle went. Tommy Pye was ambushed by female relatives: mother, auntie, gran. They surrounded him; you could hear him in the middle protesting. Seconds later he wriggled free and bolted, leaving their loving circle briefly hollow, like a human doughnut.

Mrs Pye looked puzzled.

'Puppy?' she said. 'Did he say "puppy"?'

'Yes, puppy,' said her mum.

'Puppy,' her sister said.

Mrs Pye stuck out an expert hand to grab little Albert as he went flying past. 'C'mere, you.' The puzzled look persisted on her face, joined now by a shadow of suspicion.

'What puppy?'

12

The Ball inside the Full Back

The ever-increasing variety of the town's industries augurs well for the future prosperity of Oldbury. Besides the wide range of its hardware output, from edge-tools to bicycle frames, and of its chemicals, from alkali to phosphorus, it produces blue bricks and cardboard boxes, tar, jam, and pale ale, immense engine boilers and delicate surgical dressings, and a catalogue of other manufactures equally strange in their diversity, to say nothing of the railway carriages and the canal barges by which they may be expeditiously carried away.

Frederick William Hackwood,
Oldbury and Round About (1915)

We walked home through the darkening town, up Perrott Street, round behind the covered market, past the town hall and the library, past the shops.

'I don't like it at left back,' said Graham. 'I'm better at right half, really.'

A low sulphurous fog, expelled from Danks's furnaces, fanned out across the road. Street lamps floated like jellyfish in the spooky yellowish light. The smoke stung in our noses, prickled our eyes, shortened our lives.

'I don't like it at right back,' Malcolm Prosser said.

We paused from time to time to gaze into some lighted window. Sturgess's, the butcher's, had a model of a pig in a butcher's apron waving a cleaver at us. There was the sound of singing from the Zion Chapel, set back from the road behind a wrought-iron fence and pair of gates. Singing too, and cigarette smoke from the Blue Gates pub close by. Interestingly, both establishments were adorned with stained-glass windows.

'Edna May likes it on the wing,' said Brenda, walking beside Edna May who was riding her bike. 'You should pass to her more.'

My invisible dad appeared, and soon after disappeared, on *his* bike. He tinkled his bell and waved. He'd arrived straight from work, plus overtime, five minutes before the end. Almost as shy as Mr Sorrell, he'd come up to us when the whistle went, slipped me a sixpence and melted back into the crowd.

'I'd pass to her,' said Brenda.

'I'd pass to you,' Edna May said. She pedalled up alongside Joey, who was kicking a ball in a sprout bag. 'Who we playin' next?'

We had reached the boundary of Danks's private fog and were out into clearer air. Haywood's Outfitters loomed ahead, its double window occupied by posing dummies, suits and dresses and hats, sheets, tea towels, pillowcases, school uniforms . . . and sports kit. Ten days ago half of this impressive frontage had been boarded up, the window smashed, stock removed, suspects sought. Ronnie had seen it the morning after, broken glass and splintered wood all over the pavement, blood too, Ronnie said. Dummies in even more preposterous attitudes, slumped sideways or hanging out beyond the jagged edges of the window. Blood, yes. And Rufus Toomey had that progressively dirtier bandage on his hand for days after.

'Who we playin' next?' said Edna May again.

'Aston Villa,' said Joey and flicked his sprout-bagged ball – playfully, flirtatiously – in Edna May's direction.

A pungent smell of a different sort was reaching

us now from the green and curdling waters of the Tipton canal. As we crossed the bridge, a woman came up from the towpath hauling a small boy behind her and clipping him round the head. The boy was stoical and made no sound. An elderly dog followed on at a safe distance.

Monica Copper was with us with two other girls. Their white ankle socks shone luminously in the dark. Trevor – don't ask me how, I had not told a soul, except Spencer maybe – had picked up on my partiality for Monica and was doing his best to further our romance.

'He loves you,' Trevor said. 'He said –'

'No, I never.'

'She loves him,' said one of the other girls.

'I don't!' said Monica, rather too emphatically for my liking.

'*You* love '*er*,' said Joey, joining in. But with his face in shadow it was not possible to tell who this particular attachment referred to.

The Birmingham Road was quiet; it was almost eight o'clock. Joey spilled his ball from its net and began dribbling along; passes were given and received. Spencer had dropped back and was talking to Tommy Ice Cream. Tommy had his collar up and his flat cap on. He looked like a column of cloth.

'That's the best pitch ever!' cried Ronnie, in a rare display of enthusiasm.

'I could play for always on that pitch,' agreed Arthur.

'Me too,' said Edna May.

'Not right back, though,' Malcolm said, and he produced a massive sigh. 'I don't like it.'

One more canal with its bridge and we were out and above the main cup of the town. Nowadays, 2004, at this junction the M5 thunders overhead on thirty-foot stilts. The houses that we passed that night are, most of them, still there: vibrating with the traffic, shivering like Mrs Moore.

When I arrived home the house was in darkness. Dad had left already, off to the Buffs: the Royal and Ancient Order of Buffaloes, a club for men that met every Friday night in an upstairs room at the Malt Shovel. Mum was not yet back from her work, cleaning offices. Dinah rose up from the rug, wagging her stumpy tail. I drank thirstily, straight from the tap, made myself some bread 'n' drippin' and sat for a time with the lights off, in the firelight.

In the heat of the fire my mud-slicked socks and knees were drying out. Soon little patterns and crazings would form and eggshell layers of mud would fall away. My boneless body sank into the easy chair – under extra gravity, it seemed – worn out and sore. A graze on my elbow was beginning to sting. My brain was drifting.

I felt . . . what? A wordless, *thought*less something. A sense of radiating contentment, happiness. Moves played out in my head. I could see the 3D geometry of them: the pitch, the players, the ball. Especially this: I get the ball, moving left, moving left, drawing the defenders across the pitch, then swivel and hit a twenty-yard pass with my left foot back the other way, *into space*. 'The Ball inside the Full Back', exactly as Stanley Matthews described it.

And later, drifting still: three cheers from the ever-generous Sister MacPherson and her bumble-bee team; more magical oranges from the capacious folds of Rufus Toomey's coat; Tommy Pye shadowing Joey's every move, intent on getting that puppy; a commotion, smashed glasses in the Perrott Arms; Brenda dropping hints about 'other girls getting a game'; Monica smiling, maybe, but not at me.

I go to bed, forgetting to draw the curtains, omitting to have a wash. (I'd pay for that in the morning.) A double-decker bus comes blazing past the window. I just about hear the lifted latch on the door below. Mum's home. But the sound is in my dreams already. Spencer and Tommy Ice Cream talking. Brenda in the team. That little stoical boy. I am asleep . . . well, almost. Ankle socks.

13

Mrs Purnell and the Creosoted Fence

Saturday morning and pandemonium in the street.

'Raag-aboah! Raag-aboah!'

The rag-and-bone man was out there giving away paper windmills in exchange for household scrap. Also, in certain circumstances for special items, day-old chicks! Kids, of course, are suckers for anything free. They will scramble and fight to get it, needed or not. I was supposed to be helping Mrs Moore. I had fetched a sack of coke from Russell's yard, balanced precariously on our old pram. Presently, I was drinking a glass of Vimto and eating arrowroot biscuits in Mrs Moore's kitchen. Later I would shovel the coke down the chute into the cellar. But when the cry arose, 'Raag-aboah! Raag-aboah!', it was like the Pied Piper. And I ran with all the rest.

Spencer joined me and together we ransacked the wash house and dad's shed. Elsewhere in the street other more law-abiding kids were pestering their mothers. Mine, fortunately, was out. Spencer's situation was different. His mother kept everything so spick-and-span there was nothing in their house to swap.

We gathered together a few items – tin cans, buckled bike wheel, ruined umbrella, newspapers – and stuffed them into a sack. Jack Piggott with his pony and cart was parked at the bottom of Tugg Street with a scrum of kids and a flurry of windmills around him. His pony, Monty, was tucking into a nosebag of oats and being petted half to death by the crowd. Up on the cart, in a cardboard box with little holes in it ('That's a nice cardboard box with little holes in it!') were the day-old chicks. You could hear their tiny tantalizing 'Cheep, cheeps'! I was familiar with day-old chicks. We bought them ourselves from time to time in West Bromwich market. Once, I remember, we had this chick, one of half a dozen, and it died in the kitchen, slumped forward on its beak like a book end. Mum came in from the yard, saw it and *put it in the oven.* I was horrified. Only the oven was not so hot, and the heat, as Mum intended, revived it.

What Spencer and I got from Jack Piggott were two windmills. Which pleased us at first till we realized we were too old for windmills. A day-old chick was a prize to possess; windmills were for babies.

I accompanied Spencer then to Cotterill's to get his hair cut. Mr Cotterill was hard at work; Saturday morning was his busy time. Mysteriously, he had acquired two cups of tea, one to the left of him, one to the right, from both of which he was drinking. He also had a racking cough. There was more tea in the saucers than anywhere else. The radio was on so loud conversation was impossible. The floor had disappeared under a rug of hair. Three or four smokers were assisting Mr Cotterill in obliterating the atmosphere.

In the afternoon Ronnie, Spencer and I got a fire going at the end of Ronnie's garden, which sloped away and was therefore hidden from the houses. Ronnie acquired the matches and a couple of paper bags. Spencer and I foraged around for combustible material: stuff from dustbins, twigs, an old and rotting seed tray. I had a passion for lighting fires. I would have made a good caveman. Later, Ronnie obtained a potato from the house and we tried cooking it. As time went by, other items were added to the flames: a rubber band which produced a dreadful (wonderful!) smell, a lead soldier which melted down into a blob, a tiny celluloid frog which disappeared entirely in a puff of smoke. Eventually, we ate the potato, passing it round from hand to hand. Spencer, well-mannered as always, wiped it first with his hankie. The potato was charred black on the outside, raw on the inside and delicious. I can recall the taste of it even now.

We sat on our haunches around the dying fire. Ronnie proposed that we piddle on it to put it out. For safety reasons. I made a joke about Ronnie becoming a fireman when he grew up. Spencer rubbed – thoughtfully, absent-mindedly – his cropped head, and pulled something out of the long grass.

'Hey, look at this!'

It was a rusty tin can with a wire handle.

'Mine,' said Ronnie.

What Spencer had found was a fire-can. He gave it a swing. 'Remember that time with Mrs Purnell?'

'Yeah,' said I.

'Yeah,' said Ronnie, though he as it happened had not been there.

A nosy cat came down the garden to have a look at us. A plane flew overhead. We poked the fire, resurrected it, and told ourselves, patchworking it together, the story (resurrecting *it* too) of . . .

Mrs Purnell and the Creosoted Fence. It was last year, early November and the dark nights coming. It was the season for fire-cans. A fire-can was a serious delight to me: portable fire! To make one you needed a can, a hammer, a six-inch nail, a block of wood for hammering into and wire for the handle. Then, take the can, hammer a dozen holes into it and attach the handle. Grown-ups disapproved of fire-cans and confiscated them on sight. Spencer and I hid ours behind the Bodleys' hen house.

One evening about half-past five – it was the night before bonfire night – Spencer and I were returning from Milward's with a bag of fireworks and sparklers, bought with our own money. We had stood for three nights outside the Malt Shovel with a guy in a pram. The guy was hardly more than a sack of salvage in a pair of trousers and a hat, but it had earned us three and ninepence.

The street was darkening fast. A solidifying mixture of fog and smoke was gathering above the rooftops and blocking off the ends of the street. The cemetery was invisible. We paused beneath a street lamp to admire again our collection of bangers, volcanoes and silver rain. It seems to me now I almost more loved looking at them, *reading* them, with their fairground colours and exotic names, than letting them off.

A figure loomed out at us from the entry, hesitant

and quivering. 'H-h-hallo, boys.' It was Mrs Moore – 'Evenin', Mrs Moore!' – off with her jug to the pub.

Spencer took the fireworks into his house and returned soon after with a newspaper under his coat. We drifted across the yard. The Bodleys' dog barked and rattled on its chain. The Bodleys' baby howled from an upstairs window. Behind the Bodleys' hen house we recovered our fire-cans and prepared to christen them: Spencer's paper, my matches, a previously collected stash of rabbit-hutch straw and twigs.

The theory of fire-cans was straightforward: light your fire, get it going, fill it up and swing. The rush of air acted as a bellows. In the right conditions, a well-made can would glow red hot like a furnace. Sometimes they even melted. Sometimes sparks flew and boys set light to themselves. Eyebrows and even eyes were lost.

This time we were more in danger of choking to death. Smoke was considerable, but flames were few. The twigs were too green and sappy.

'Come on!' I headed back up the yard.

'Where we going?'

Crouching down, I scuttled along behind the row of wash houses. Spencer followed.

'Where we –'

'Sh!'

Mrs Purnell's was where we were going. She had a fence of loosely slatted creosoted boards around one section of her garden to keep the dogs off. What she grew there, I cannot recall.

It was getting darker and foggier all the time. Blurred squares of light glowed out across the yard from various windows; a cloud of steam from the open lighted window of the Fogartys' wash house; an expanse of lighted roof from the Creda.

On hands and knees we crept up to the Purnells' fence. Nervous hens clucked nearby. *They* knew we were there.

Spencer whispered hoarsely. 'I don't like this.'

I pulled hard on a board.

'I think we should . . .'

It wouldn't budge.

'Let's *go*!'

I tried another. The Bodleys' baby was still bawling. A car horn sounded in the street. The board creaked horribly and split; half of it came away in my hand. I fell back on to Spencer, who was crouched behind me. Then – bang! – the nearest lavatory door flew open and a dreadful, raving apparition with a torch was on us. I was grabbed, half throttled, dragged to my feet and yelled at.

'That's my fence, y'little bugger!'

It was Mrs Purnell. She snatched the stolen board, threw it down and landed me a fearful swipe to the head.

'I'll teach you!'

Back I tumbled on to Spencer again. He yelled, I yelled, Mrs Purnell was still yelling, the hens were going mad and a pink-faced Mrs Fogarty was shouting questions from her wash-house window.

Mrs Purnell hauled me up again. Spencer, she ignored. He could have run but chose to stay.

'I'll give you bonfires!'

She was a mighty woman, half as big again as my mother, but, as it turned out, not so tough.

Mum was there, in her apron and one slipper. 'Hey!' She grabbed my arm and pulled me free. Mrs Purnell advanced. Mum stood firm.

'Bloody kids!'

'*My* kids,' said Mum, briefly, it seems, adopting Spencer. 'Hit your own.'

Unpersuaded, Mrs Purnell tried to wallop me again. 'Bloody bonfires!'

I was tucked in behind my mother, with Spencer (shivering) behind me. Mrs Purnell sought to hit us with the broken board.

'Hey!' Mum grabbed the board and hit her with it.

Mrs Purnell dropped her torch, staggered back against the fence and – 'Bloody cow!' – retreated.

It was over. Mum shepherded us across the yard. Mrs Purnell's parting insults were ignored, and Mrs Fogarty's pleas for information. Spencer came to our house to clean himself up before going home. I could taste blood in my mouth. The stinging pattern of Mrs Purnell's fingers was visible still as I gazed at myself in the bluebird mirror. Presently, as the pain faded and Spencer left, I began to consider my alibi.

14

Mr Cork, Mr Skidmore and Mrs Glue

On Monday morning in assembly Mr Reynolds was so cheerful he looked ready to float away. His smile shone down on us like the sun. We were all his friends at that moment, every one of us, even Amos. (Pear drops all round and no cane.) The 'A' team had hammered Tabernacle Street 9–2. This was a doubly satisfying result for Mr Reynolds. The headmaster of Tabernacle Street was Mr Gittings. He and Mr Reynolds had been students together at the same college. Their rivalry was ancient and unceasing. So, well, yippee, hooray and goodbye Tabernacle Street. What's more, amazingly, other boys from this school and – goodness me! – one girl had also achieved great things. Now to cap it all, they were to play each other – 'Sh!' – yes, play each other in the semi-finals.

The players were invited to stand up and take a bow. A wave of shyness washed over me and my face felt hot. Ronnie looked cool; Edna May was smiling confidently around. Spencer, our ever-modest manager, remained seated. Mr Reynolds, glowing like a lamp, continued to speak for some time, concentrating now on the quality of coaching going on, and indeed that Rood End Primary was justly famous for. Mr Cork was invited to take a bow. It startled me, I recall, to see how even this fierce man was affected by such public praise and the ragged cheers that accompanied it. He flushed and waved his solitary arm like a man bothered with bees.

Mr Reynolds in this particular assembly made no mention of Jesus or any goings-on in the toilets. All the same, the otherwise happy scene was blighted in the end. Children, when gathered together in any numbers, have a natural instinct for chaos. They can sense the possibility of it, like a dog anticipating a walk. Thus it was that ripples of movement – nudging, elbowing, *pinching* – arose, accompanied by an expanding hubbub. Mr Reynolds, his smile switched off, was required to quench things.

While we were on our feet being congratulated, I'd found myself right next to Amos and Vincent Loveridge. It occurred to me, and to the rest of us I'll bet, to wonder how ever we could beat this lot.

(Amos assured me out of the corner of his mouth that they would 'marmalize' us.) Look at them: Ackerman, Briggs, Tommy Gray; Amos, broad and solid like a barrel . . . and Vincent. Vincent Loveridge really was the most admired boy in the school in those days. Captain of football, captain of cricket, captain of tiddlywinks, if we'd had one. He looked like a movie star; all the girls loved him. If I'd been a girl, I'd have loved him. He was a rough boy, though, like the rest of us; lived in a terrace, dad a foundryman. And yet to see him, head held high, wavy light brown hair, blue eyes – you could have stuck a top hat on his head and sent him to Eton.

But that's enough of them; forget the opposition. Boy for boy, they might have the better players, but football when you get down to it is a team game, isn't it? Team spirit and all that. Besides, we had tactics. Since beating St Saviour's, Spencer had had us practising all kinds of stuff: free kicks, corners, lining up in a wall. Offside as well. Spencer had borrowed a referee's handbook from the library. Using his chalks in Joey's yard, he had demonstrated the offside law so effectively that even the Prossers got it. Offside means, you see, that basically if your defence pushes up, their attackers have to retreat, otherwise – offside! It squashes them in. Mr Cork's idea of tactics was more military than anything. Boot the ball as far as you could and run after it. Up and at 'em. I'm exaggerating perhaps.

As for the players themselves, our players that is, well, startling improvements were there for all to see.

(1) Tommy Ice Cream. Tommy was coming out of himself. Often now he'd walk along with us in the street. His conversation was restricted – 'Yeth' and 'Noth' mainly – but it was an advance on grunting. A couple of times he had been observed to laugh. Spencer had a way with him. Tommy still had bouts of bad temper and stubbornness, taking offence, refusing to let go of the ball, but Spencer could usually calm him down. Tommy's amazing kicking power, one end of the pitch to the other, was an asset. His throwing too, when you could ever get him to do it.

(2) Malcolm Prosser. Malcolm, on the other hand, had gone back into himself. He continued to complain about playing right back, missed the company of a brother complaining about playing left back and, I suspect, was peeved to be lining up with a sister who was better than he was.

(3) Graham Glue. Graham had something of his dad's gloominess about him. He had a phobia about getting his shorts dirty. But he was a tackler, and quick, and though he didn't particularly care to pass the ball, could often be persuaded – 'Bloody *pass* it' – to do so.

(4) Trevor Darby. Another quick tackler. Trevor was a terrier, really. Off the pitch forever ferreting around to find out who loved who, on the pitch forever ferreting after the ball. He muttered to himself a good deal under his breath, urging himself on. He had a little sister, Dorothy, who he had trained to drop Dolly Mixtures into his open mouth at half-time while he lay on the ground pretending to be dying. This gave him extra energy, he claimed. Like most of the team, he had a clear bias against any form of passing. The introduction of Edna May on the wing, however, brought about a change of heart. She could get passes off him. Trevor (secretly!) admired Edna May, while loudly proclaiming that Joey loved her.

(5) Joey Skidmore. Joey was the rock of the team. He held the defence together and, often as not, the attack too. I've mentioned before the courage required to head one of those lead-weighted leather

balls we played with. Well, Joey was a master at it. He *had* the courage, that's the trick, to attack the ball, face up to it, like advancing on a hostile dog or rhino. In these circumstances, apparently – I was no good at it myself – courage was rewarded. It hurt less.

(6) Arthur Toomey. Talking of huge improvements, Arthur was a good example. For a start he turned out to be naturally two-footed. He could beat his man, he could and would pass the ball, and run into space and pass it again. After me, I'd say, Arthur was the most thoughtful player in the team. He was assuredly the smartest dresser. His kit, when he stepped on to the pitch, was immaculate, in sharp contrast to his normal appearance. He slicked his hair down with a wet comb and combed it again at half-time. He looked like Stanley Matthews or the boy dummy in Haywood's window.

(7) Edna May Prosser. The thing about Edna May was, she was a natural. Tommy Pye was a natural, Albert Pye even more of a natural, but that was just football. Edna May was easygoing, relaxed, adventurous – in everything. When she stood up and smiled around in the hall, she wasn't showing

off, or being modest, or pretending to be modest, she was being herself. Natural. Her football skills were limited but effective. She had a good right foot, a keen eye; she could see a pass and was prepared to suffer – tackles, shoulder charges and such – when the need arose. Overall she enjoyed the game and did not flinch.

(8) Me.

> What I like best, yes most of all
> In my whole life, is kicking a ball.
>
> *Heard it in the Playground* (1989)

That's me, in a nutshell. I had this bald, mouldy-looking tennis ball which I dribbled with on the way to school till it disappeared down a drain. I even had a ball that I'd made myself out of cut-up rings from an inner tube wrapped round a core of silver-paper sweet wrappers. It was hardly bigger than a golf ball and bounced about, all that rubber, like a live thing. I kicked a ball in the playground, the park, the back yard, the street, the cemetery even, one time. Balls I kicked ended up in other people's gardens and front rooms, under lorries, floating off down rivers and canals, carried off triumphantly in dogs' mouths, confiscated by teachers. As far as my contribution to the team went, I had a good engine and could run forever. I was the only one of us who got to enjoy passing, preferred it almost, feinting to run with it, threading it through. I linked things up between attack and defence. Oh yes, and I was the captain.

(9) Ronnie Horsfield. Ronnie was a puzzle. A player who advised other players without doing all that much himself. A centre forward who didn't score many. He had a good kick on him and his noisy, confident manner drew defenders towards him, leaving gaps for Wyatt and Tommy Pye to exploit. All the same, how Ronnie ever got to play in the most popular position, being as he was just about the least effective player, is a mystery. As I recall, when we had the vote for who'd be captain, he nearly won that. There again, his confidence had its uses. In the changing rooms and walking out on to the pitch, while some of us might secretly doubt our chances and glance uneasily (admiringly) at the opposition, Ronnie strode forth to victory. The other team could as well go home. Ronnie's message, like Amos's, was emphatic: we'll marmalize ya.

(10) Tommy Pye. Tommy was our best player and he was only seven, and that's not the half of it. He

was getting better day by day, hour by hour! I'm not exaggerating. He was like a little overnight mushroom sprouting upwards. He had this round chubby face and chubby knees, but give him a ball and he was like a whippet. That's it, he was a mushroom and a whippet. When Spencer told us stuff, the offside rule, for instance, Tommy took it all in. It was as though Spencer was merely reminding him of things he already knew. Sometimes kids come along who can do things so effortlessly, so instantaneously, it looks like reincarnation. Tommy was one of these. Nor was his size a total disadvantage. His centre of gravity was so low you had little hope of knocking him off the ball. He was like a mushroom, a whippet and one of the lead-weighted dolls you put in a canary's cage for it to play with. He could come in under the other team's radar too.

(11) Wyatt. I've been trying to remember Wyatt's other name. I'm almost certain it was Robert: i.e. Bob. It's a funny thing about names. Some kids – Amos, Ackerman, Wyatt – were always known to one and all by a single name. Others, Ronnie Horsfield, Vincent Loveridge, got both, and Edna May Prosser all three. Even the teachers followed this rule. I bet even the vicars did: I christen this

baby . . . Amos. Wyatt was a special player too. He had a long, loping stride and a lovely left foot. When he didn't have the ball, he took his ease out on the wing like someone in the Bandstand Café waiting to be served. When he did have it, he ran. Wyatt had confidence, like Ronnie, though in his case it was more specific. Give him the ball, wait a while and pick it out of the back of the net. He never expected not to score, consequently he'd never pass to you, that would be an admission of failure. Playing on the wing suited him; open spaces from which to run at defences and a touchline full of interesting people to chat with and keep informed about his latest bath or haircut.

(Secretary/Manager) Spencer Sorrell. Spencer was, I realize now, the rarest of us. His soccer skills were limited but his social skills were immense. The others, me included, were rowdy savages most of the time, pilferers and piddlers-up-walls. Spencer was self-effacing and civilized, like a missionary among us, though he never preached. Spencer was a useful negotiator with the adults. He was, of course, drowned out in team debates about tactics and so on. But when the din died down, often as not the conclusions we reached were his. He was a good friend, as I have said, to Tommy Ice Cream,

and a better, *best* true friend to me. (He could have run, but chose to stay.)

That day, that Monday, must have been the best of my life so far. I sailed through lessons and playtimes as cheerful as Mr Reynolds. At dinner-time a little kid came up and asked me for my autograph, only Ronnie and Spencer had put him up to it. Mr Cork banged around with his cricket stump in the afternoon, made sarcastic remarks, but in an almost smiling (for him) way. For once he didn't scare me. Later on Mum was in a good mood, Dad came home early and let me have a go with his fretsaw. We had a practice session in the park. Monica Copper was there to watch.

Then, Tuesday evening – half-past seven – disaster.

Spencer, Ronnie and I went round to Graham's. He had not showed up for training. (Spencer had arranged a practice match against Leatherland's lot.) When we got there, a smashed plate with the remains of somebody's dinner – pork chop, gravy, peas – was out in the yard and the back door was open. In the kitchen Mrs Glue was over by the sink, shivering and wiping her eyes with her apron. Graham, white-faced, was beside her. Upstairs a great banging and clattering and shouting and swearing . . . from Mr Glue.

We never got the whole story till much later. It turned out Mr Glue was enraged by something his mates at work had told him about Mrs Glue. He had come home and thrown his dinner out the back door. He had also, apparently, hit Mrs Glue and knocked her over. Graham got in between them and his dad hit him as well. Now Mr Glue was upstairs packing a suitcase, for himself or Mrs Glue it wasn't clear.

What Mr Glue had heard was that Mrs Glue had been seen in the Blue Gates two nights previously having half a pint of shandy with *Mr* Skidmore, and that this was not the only occasion the two of them had shared a drink. Mrs Glue said it was the only occasion; she had been waiting to meet her friend, she said. It was Mr Glue's nature, though, to assume the worst; trust his mates and doubt his wife.

Well, this was a bad business for the Glue family, but (of course, *we* thought) a worse business for us. Mr Glue had prevented Graham from coming to training and banned him from playing in the team, altogether, forever. No son of his, he yelled for half the street to hear, was playing around with any ragged-arsed, snotty-nosed, chicken-livered son of Skidmore's!

We stood, me, Ronnie, Spencer, transfixed in the kitchen like witnesses at a road accident. Mrs Glue was in shock, Graham's eyes were brimful of tears, their old cat, Ruby, crouched fur on end like a porcupine under the sink.

Mr Glue thundered back downstairs and burst into the kitchen empty-handed. 'And another thing!' he yelled, advancing on Mrs Glue, who flinched and clutched Graham tightly to her, so tightly, I noticed, that his mouth was squashed into a pathetic mournful 'O'. Mr Glue saw us then. Spencer bravely attempted some polite words; Ronnie for once was at a loss. Mr Glue was having none of it. 'You lot,' he said, almost conversationally and wafting his hand. 'Sod off.'

15

The Boys from the Bottom Pitch

'Brenda!

Brenda could play!

Pick 'er – she's a . . .

She's a good 'un!'

We were in the sheds again, out of the rain again, the wind blowing in off the pockmarked pond. This 'pond', by the way, was bigger than you might imagine, a hundred and fifty yards by eighty at least; more of a lake, really. A brook flowed into it at one end and waterfalled out of it the other. There was a substantial island in the middle with trees and nesting ducks and moorhens on it. There was a boathouse (haunted) which hired out rowing boats and canoes. A lone rower was visible now in the grey and drizzly air. Mr Bissell or his brother, probably, the boathouse owners.

Ronnie, I might add, was permanently be-witched by that island and ever wanted to set foot on it and poke around. It was his Shangri-La. He paddled out in a canoe one time, but got yelled at by one of the Mr Bissells: 'Come in, number nine!' Finally, I heard, when he was thirteen or so, he walked over one frozen winter and got marooned for half a day when the ice cracked. I wish I had been there to see it.

Edna May, oblivious to the weather, was circling the sheds on her bike, offering with each circuit her opinion on team selection.

'Brenda, Brenda!'

We were discussing Graham's replacement. He had not come to school today, it was Wednesday evening now, the match was tomorrow. Mr Glue had been seen glaring out of their front-room window, but of Graham and his mother there was no sign.

Spencer was the obvious replacement, had to be. But Spencer was absent (accordion lesson), together with Tommy Pye (determined mother), Tommy Ice Cream (not known) and Wyatt (manicure? hairdresser?). The conversation, which needed to be serious, got away from us. Joey brought up Albert Pye again, Tommy's five-year-old – 'No, six!' – baby brother.

'Maybe Albert's got a baby brother,' said Trevor.

'Or sister!' Edna May called out.

'The Smiths' baby's pretty good, I heard,' said I.

'Let's pick Archie!' cried Ronnie.

Archie was under the seat with a revoltingly dirty bone, a gift from an admirer.

'Archie's a good 'un.'

'Brenda is!'

'Could you pick a dog?' said Prosser (Malcolm) seriously.

'Why not?' said Ronnie. 'There's nothin' in the rules against it.'

'There's nothin' in the rules against pickin' a chicken!' yelled Trevor.

'Or a gorilla,' said Prosser (Patrick).

'Archie, Archie!' cried Joey, getting at this point too close to Archie and his beloved bone.

Archie stiffened and growled.

'That'd be a team,' cried Trevor. 'Boys, girls, babies – and a dog.'

Suddenly, there was Tommy Ice Cream, the rain dripping down off his hat, nose, chin. Once more the conversation veered away. Joey was interested in the mystery of the shirts. It *had* to be the Toomeys: past history, bloody bandage, they probably pinched the oranges too. There again, Arthur said Rufus had told him they knew nothing about it. He'd cut his hand on a tin-opener, Arthur said. So maybe . . .

'Tommy?' said Joey, leaning out into the rain. 'Got y'jersey on?'

Tommy lowered his head and peeked inside his coat. 'Noth.'

'Did y'dad get y'that jersey?'

'Yeth.' Tommy shuffled uneasily. This was an extended conversation for him.

'Did he, er, get the shirts?'

Tommy ducked his head again. He well knew what was what. Joey had been down this road before; Ronnie and Wyatt likewise. Even so, I think the question confused him. Maybe he thought we thought his dad ought to have got the shirts. I don't know. Tommy retreated, nearly colliding with Edna May – a drowned rat! – on one of her circuits. A rumble of thunder rolled in above the boathouse, wind ruffled the already choppy waters of the pond. Archie grabbed up his bone and departed.

'Yeth,' said Tommy. 'Noth.'

THE OLDBURY AND DISTRICT
QUEEN ELIZABETH II CORONATION CUP

SEMI-FINAL: MALT SHOVEL ROVERS V.
ROOD END PRIMARY 'A'

VENUE: GKN SPORTS GROUND
DATE: 16 APRIL 1953

KICK-OFF: 5.30 P.M.

The Team

Goalkeeper	Thomas Capanelli
Right back	Malcolm Prosser
Left back	Spencer Sorrell
Right half	Trevor Darby
Centre half	Joey Skidmore
Left half	Arthur Toomey
Outside right	Edna May Prosser
Inside right	Me
Centre forward	Ronnie Horsfield
Inside left	Tommy Pye
Outside left	Wyatt

On Thursday evening at a quarter to five we took the familiar walk: Rood End Road, Oldbury Road, Birmingham Road to Guest, Keen & Nettlefold's sports ground. The Boys from the Bottom Pitch all set to play (and marmalize) the boys from the top. We were early; no way we'd be late. Even so a few spectators, dogs and a groundsman were there before us.

The top pitch was a sight to see, its lines so crisp and white, its grass so green. The rollers and metal drums had been tidied away. Ladies from GKN's canteen were setting up a refreshment stall in front of the pavilion. The sky was the clearest blue, the air pleasantly warm, and if it ponged a bit, with a plastics factory one side and a glue factory the other, we were used to it. Along the horizon tall factory chimneys puffing away. The Tipton canal beyond the bottom fence, you could see its bridges. A rhythmic thumping and clanging from Crosby's sheet metal works a hundred yards away.

We were early; Edna May was earlier, sitting on her bike leaning against the pavilion. Joey was all for having a kick-about, but Spencer urged us to save our energy. Anyway that groundsman – kids with *no* adult? – had his eye on us. We entered the pavilion, cool and dusty like a chapel, and sat down on its narrow benches. We were, all of us, all of a sudden subdued. Wyatt produced a sandwich, Trevor a bottle of pop. It came home to me then, one more match and we'd be *in the final.* Sixteen teams – well, fifteen really, Rolfe Street had had a bye in the first round – and now there were only four. Well, three really. Rounds Green had won their semi-final last night down at Perrott Street. Prosser (Patrick) had watched the second half; no great shakes, in his opinion. We'd marmalize 'em.

It was quiet. Tommy Ice Cream had begun to hum to himself, which he did on occasion. We could hear Amos and the others next door, their clattering boots and voices, Mr Cork's deep growl. And outside too, a growing hubbub. Mr Ash poked his head round the door, nodded and withdrew. Brenda tapped on the window and Edna May went out to speak to her. Spencer held up the white shirt he'd be wearing and asked for our opinions. Would it do, did we think? Would the ref allow it? Then the door swung open again and in came Mrs Glue, with Graham close behind.

Mrs Glue was pale and nervous. There again, looking back, it seems to me now we were all pale and nervous, though not any more.

'Gray!'

'Gray!'

'Graham!'

'Gluey!'

Apart from yelling Graham's name, leaping around in the confined space, knocking a bench over, spilling Trevor's pop, little or nothing was said (embarrassment, shyness, on all sides). Mrs Glue took Graham's shirt out of her shopping bag. Apparently, showing great courage, she had gone back to the house, confronting Mr Glue, to get it. She gave Graham a hugely sloppy kiss – more embarrassment – hugged him and left.

16

Come Bloody On

So Hurrah for the Old Boys of Oldbury,
Who have built up the fame of our School,
For they played the game, we must do the same,
Until all hail the fair name of Oldbury.
Though the strife of life may be swift and keen,
Though we may find hard knocks to rule,
Heed not the praise or blame, carry on
and play the game,
For we are boys (girls) of Oldbury School.

Oldbury Grammar School Song

My recollection of these boyhood days is extraordinarily complete, intense and reliable. And yet I know it isn't – reliable, that is. I have trouble with Wyatt's other name, can't picture the front garden of our house at all or remember whether Mrs Moore had a husband or not. Also, take old man Cutler and his bonfires. It seems to me he had one going all the time, summer and winter, rain or shine. But think about it: whatever could he find to burn? Or again, the shirts. It never bothered us that they were almost certainly pinched. But what about our parents? Wouldn't some of them ask questions? Not in my recollection they didn't.

Anyway, back to the match, that semi-final, which, all the same and nevertheless, I remember. It is engraved on my brain. Plug me into a monitor and you could see it all. Even my feet – especially my feet – remember it.

We stepped out on to the pitch in better spirits than seemed possible half an hour ago. Graham's return had given us a double lift. We had him back and Spencer back, as manager. The noisy crowd pressed in on every side – pity the poor linesmen – a great gathering of parents, kids and dogs. My Uncle Ike was there ('C'mon, our Allan!'), accompanying his older brother, my shy and silent father, George Henry. Mr Cork and Mr Reynolds, of course; Mr and Mrs Cotterill. Half of Rounds Green's team, there to spy on the opposition. Some of the canteen ladies come to see what all the fuss was about. Contrasting tribes of Ackermans (respectable) and

Toomeys (not). Babes in arms and prams. Ice Cream Jack.

First half. It was a game of eleven goals and we scored all eleven – one each. No, not really. I don't, worse luck, remember *that.* No, five minutes after the kick-off, following our usual start, it was 2–0 to them: a thumping shot from Tommy Gray and a scrambled, bulldozing effort – the ball ping-ponging around in the goalmouth – from Amos. In each case their tactics were the same: a big boot upfield and a cavalry charge. We were in disarray. It could've been three or four. Tommy Ice Cream hurled himself about and blocked or deflected goal-bound shots and headers, from Gray again and Charlie Cotterill. Joey headed off the line. Rutter hit a post.

Meanwhile, Vincent Loveridge was cool and elegant at centre half, Amos strutted cockily in midfield, Tommy Gray was flying down the wing, and they were all over us. It was a piece of cake, wasn't it? We were the odds and sods, not even the 'B' team. Mr Cork looked smug on the line. Mr Reynolds, his hands wrapped round a mug of tea, was relaxed.

Lining up for the restart after Amos's goal, a scowling Ronnie poked me in the ribs with his elbow.

'C'mon,' he said, glaring back at Joey and the others. 'C'mon. Come bloody on.'

'Language, language,' said the ref.

Ronnie glared at him. He pushed the ball to Tommy Pye . . . and we came on.

Tommy Pye – what a little angel! – beloved of the crowd in his yet voluminous shirt, marooned as it seemed in the land of giants out there on that enormous pitch – bamboozled Rutter and Charlie Cotterill, got to the byline, whacked a low cross with bewildering power into the goalmouth, where Ronnie arriving late, all four limbs flailing away like a combine harvester, collided with the ball and kneed it like a bullet past Ackerman's unseeing gaze.

'C'mon, c'mon!' cried Ronnie, grabbing the ball from the bulging net. And we came again.

Spirits lifted, we had begun to find our passing game. Arthur and me combined in a couple of push and runs.

'Stop faffin' about!' yelled Mr Skidmore.

Like a human zipper, we zipped past Rutter and Higgs and set Wyatt free on the left. He strode away, hammered a shot against a post and, with Ackerman flat out having dived to make the save, up popped Arthur again to poke it home.

The crowd was going, there's no other word for

it, wild. Mr Cork was red-faced and yelling, insults mostly, at his own team. Something I haven't mentioned so far, our offside studies were beginning to pay dividends. Spencer had Joey and the others pushing up; Tommy Gray, especially, was offside pretty well every time he got the ball. Mr Cork, luckily without his cricket stump, was outraged. I suspect he saw this as a form of cheating. His brave, vaulting cavalry brought constantly to a halt by a measly whistle. Our supporters were in good heart. Brenda and her older sisters had acquired a collection of ancient football rattles which they vigorously wielded. The Toomeys – with a rare sighting of Mrs Toomey plus baby, and Mr Toomey minus shirt (just jacket and vest) – were a small, vociferous crowd in themselves. Uncle Ike was advising one and all, but mainly me, on the finer points. 'Get after 'im, our kid, he couldn't trap a bag o' sand!'

They came back at us; laid siege to our goal and might have scored a couple of times. Suddenly and surprisingly in so congested and fast-moving a scene, there was Amos with the ball on his own not ten yards out. He picked his spot, swung his leg and – whoosh! – in came Tommy Pye – him again, he could do it all – took the ball clean off Amos's toe. Amos, committed whole-heartedly to his follow-through, followed through and swung himself right off his feet. By the time he was up again, the ball was down the other end in the back of the net. And Prosser (Malcolm) it was – our out-of-position, undisciplined, unwilling ('I don't like it at right back') right back – who scored.

Half-time. 3–2 to us (unbelievable), five goals gone, six to go. Rufus and Albert produced their lovely hoard of oranges. Albert flourished his evil-looking knife and showed off, for some reason, an air pistol. Mrs Pye went to work on Tommy's face with her hankie. Ice Cream Jack ventured to join us. Brenda and her rattling sisters. Mrs Glue with a darkly bruised cheek, but looking more cheerful. Out on the pitch a few of the dads were kicking about. Uncle Ike in his green gasworks overalls was dodging around in the penalty area, doffing his cap.

'On me 'ead, Lenny! On me 'ead!'

I spotted Mr Loveridge, a modest little walnut-faced man gazing up at his tall son. However could the one be the father of the other, you had to wonder. It was like a fairy tale. Vincent surely had been spirited away as a baby. His actual father surely, surely, was a duke.

Mr and Mrs Cotterill, accompanied by their

huge and hairy dog, another Rufus (don't ask me to explore the similarities), were in a huddle with their son, Charlie. Mrs Cotterill was feeding him crisps. Mr Cotterill was hanging on to Rufus. This dog, it was believed, also got his hair cut by Mr Cotterill. Kids claimed to have seen him late at night sitting up in the chair. Same clippers as he used on us, I wouldn't be surprised.

Spencer, meanwhile, had us in a huddle.

'We're gonna win this,' said Joey.

'Tommy, throw the ball to Al, if you see him,' said Spencer.

'If I'm on me own,' said I.

'Yeth,' Tommy said.

'Tommy,' Trevor lowered his voice, 'sit on Amos.'

'If he falls over,' Graham said.

'In the goalmouth!' cried Joey.

'Noth,' Tommy said, and was that a smile?

'Flatten 'im,' said Edna May.

Second half. The first half had been played at a furious pace, the second just got furiouser. It reminds me now of a piece of classical music, by Brahms I think it was. He wrote instructions on the score how to play it: fast – faster – as fast as you can. And then, a little later – faster still! Yes, it was like that. Thirty minutes each way we played, but it felt like thirty seconds. Well, they scored (3–3), a big brave header from Vincent, and scored again (3–4), more skill from Tommy Gray. And we scored (4–4), a Joey header, and they scored (4–5), Rutter, a lucky deflection. And they hit a post and we hit a post, and it was the same post – a near own-goal from Graham. And the clock ticked on, whizzed round, and the sun declined and the sky was an ever darkening shade, lights came on in the nearby office buildings where the cleaners, my mum among them, were hard at work. And the referee looked at his watch. And we were going to lose.

Edna May, who'd had a solid game, picked up a loose ball and ran through the middle, reached Wyatt with a pass and he was off. Wyatt was difficult to tackle; tall and bony, he ran with a high knee action like a giraffe. Rutter tackled him and bounced off him. Higgs tackled him and missed. Charlie Cotterill tackled him, collided with him more like, and knocked him flying. Now, for a split second, the clock stopped. There was the smallest sliver of silence in the crowd, before the uproar. The players one and all turned their hopes and fears towards the referee.

'Penalty!'

*

I took the penalties, scored one already, as you may recall, in the Tividale match. Usually I sought to deceive the goalie, send him one way and the ball the other. On this occasion, though . . .

Ackerman stood on his line. Disconcertingly, about fifteen members of his extended family stood with him behind the goal and on either side. Worse still, all of them, every single one, had more or less *the same face;* the same round poppy eyes, the same sad, sweet, amiable expression. There was a dominant gene in there somewhere, I guess. Or God kept coming along stamping the identical design – like a pastry cutter – down on to the Ackerman baby-dough faces. It was like being asked to score against a family photograph, a tribe of goalies, all of whom – worser still – looked so mournful, you hardly had the heart to do it.

I stepped back. The crowd was hushed again; dogs barked, a baby laughed, Uncle Ike offered last-minute advice. I stepped up and hit the ball with all my might . . . straight at Ackerman.

17

Visible on Mars

Expectations in stories and books are unavoidable, aren't they? As in life. In life we peer up ahead, down the road, trying to catch a glimpse of what's in store, wondering. With a book, of course, you can flip the pages, sneak a look. You can tell when you're near or not near 'The End' by the number of pages remaining. You must be expecting now, it's only natural, for us to win: semi-final, final, cup, the lot. Why else would I write the book, tell the story? Well, as Tommy Ice Cream might have said, 'Yeth . . . and noth.' It's more complicated than it seems.

I took the kick, straight at Ackerman. He, meanwhile, hurled himself with all *his* might out of the way, diving to where he thought the ball would go.

'Goal!'

The desperate disappointment on the Ackerman family face was huge, visible on Mars. Our team celebrations were huge; no hugging or kissing, though, as previously explained.

Extra time (5–all). It was another cock-up in the Parks and Cemeteries department. The half-past five kick-off made no allowance for the possibility of extra time, ten minutes each way. We should've kicked off at five or five fifteen. Anyway, there we were, lining up once more in the gathering gloom. Matches flared on the touchlines as cigarettes and pipes were lit, traffic blazed on the Birmingham Road, the sky was an ever deeper blue with a line of rusty red and duck-egg green over the Rounds Green hills.

But we played. Truth is, we were not unused to such conditions. Our games in Albert Park often only stopped when Mr Phipps or the park bell drove us out. On winter evenings we played in the street with just a street lamp for illumination, or car headlight! So, ten minutes each way. I guess by now we must have been slowing down, but it didn't feel like it. We were steaming like horses and yelling to each other, playing by sound as much as sight, while the crowd groaned and whistled and crept ever further out on to the pitch itself, gazing after the ball. Vincent Loveridge had cut his head scoring that goal and had a plaster over his eyebrow. He looked more debonair than ever, like Errol Flynn, if you have heard of him. Amos was rampaging around in a swarm of swearwords, getting chastised, 'Language, language', by the referee.

And it got darker still. And Malcolm headed (or got his head in the way of) a fierce shot from Rutter. The ball rebounded for a throw-in! Malcolm ended up in the back of the net stunned, *concussed.* He was carried off and tended to by his frantic mother and auntie; got a face-licking later on from Rufus – the dog, that is, not Toomey. Down to ten men but it hardly mattered. The pitch was shrinking as the crowd snuck in; time was trickling if not water-falling away. Tick, tick. And now the sky was seeping into the earth, the horizon gone, no colour whatsoever in the grass. A flurry of starlings swooped and wheeled above us. Things became mysterious.

With a minute to go, the ball arrived in Tommy Ice Cream's hands. He held on to it for a moment. 'Belt it, Tommy!' yelled Spencer from behind the goal. Then, more softly, 'Belt it.'

Tommy belted it, whereupon it rose high into the night and disappeared. Players ran here and there, peering anxiously upwards like Chicken-

Licken, colliding, some of ’em. And down it came – that ball, that lovely ball! – bounced once over Tommy Gray and once again over the advancing Ackerman, and . . . where was it?

It was like the SPOT THE BALL competition in the *Sports Argus*, though by now it was so dark you could’ve played spot the players, spot the pitch. Where *was* it? And then we spotted it.

‘It’s in the net.’ (Wonder.)

‘Ref, ref!’

‘It’s in the net!’

The referee approached the near-invisible goal, bent low, squinted and blew his whistle.

It was in the net.

18

The Boy Who Went Berserk

> The most common torture is to 'do a barley-sugar', also expressed verbally in the threat 'I'll barley-sugar you', which is to twist a person's arm round until it hurts, usually behind his back, so that the sufferer has – according to which way his arm is being twisted – to lean backwards or bend forwards excessively to alleviate the pain, and is thus utterly at his tormentor's mercy. The hold is also known as 'Red hot poker', 'Fireman's torture', and 'Nelson's grip'.
>
> Iona and Peter Opie,
> *The Lore and Language of Schoolchildren* (1959)

I will tell you now the best, most memorable part of this whole business, this boyhood of mine. It was the Friday, the day following our famous victory. I was in Tugg Street on my way back from running an errand for Mrs Moore. Six o'clock or so. Soot in the air from a chimney on fire. A light drizzle falling. In Tugg Street, yes, with a sack of firewood, separate bundles, that is, bound with wire. Not so heavy, but lumpy and awkward to carry. I had paused to adjust my load while gazing into Starkey's window. And somebody passed me in the street. And spoke.

The day had begun, in my case, at six in the morning. There was no way I could sleep. I was up and, rarest of events, having breakfast with my dad. He was a fitter's mate at Crosby's, a labourer really; his hourly rate so pitifully low he had to put in all the hours God sent – a million a year! – to make a living wage. Even then we needed Mum's living wage to get by.

My Dad. A labourer, yes, but the possessor of delicate skills nonetheless. His hobby was fretwork. Late evening and into the night he would cut out the most intricate designs in wood with his treadle-operated fretsaw, glasses on the end of his nose, peering like a professor. (I still have a sewing basket that he made for Mum.) He made lead soldiers too, horsemen and such, pouring the molten metal into moulds, painting their uniforms and features with the steadiest hand and the finest brush. He made them for me.

It was a dazzling morning. I took Dinah up the park and we were so early the gates were still locked. We had to burrow our way in through a gap in the hedge. The park looked altogether unused, still in its cellophane wrapping of dew. Ducks, heads under their wings, dreamed away at the edge of the untouched and slightly steaming pond, till Dinah's lumbering attentions sent them quacking and splashing away. I sat in the sheds eating a lukewarm sausage, gift from Dad. Dinah looked hopeful but didn't get any. I climbed a tree or two; the season for climbing trees was fast approaching. Climbed *the* tree, probably, walking up it a little way, at least, for the view.

On the way to school with Spencer and Joey we gradually accumulated a gang of 'supporters', mainly infants, all frothing over at any excuse for wildness. I experienced again that curious mixture of feelings: pride, exhilaration, shyness. After the match, Mr Cork, with a face like a brick wall, had come charging into our changing room. We flinched, half expecting a cricket stump to come crashing down. Whereupon, with what might have been a smile and looking distinctly embarrassed himself, he mumbled something, shook hands with Wyatt and patted Tommy Pye on the head. Mr Reynolds was behind him in the doorway. 'Yes, well done, lads!' he called out. 'And lasses!' added Mrs Prosser, behind him.

Friday morning, then, and so much to talk about (all of it already talked about) and talk about again. We needed to *hear* it, this story of ours, from each other, from ourselves. Hold it in our minds, shore it up against the never-ending onslaught of events, the wear and tear of time.

'That goal of Tommy's!'

'Which Tommy?'

'Which goal?'

'A bomb from the skies, my uncle called it.'

'Spencer told 'im to do it.'

'That header of Malky's!'

'Knocked 'im flyin'!'

'Knocked 'im out.'

'Knocked them out . . . sort of.'

We were running the film in our heads, comparing the versions, and backwards, so it seemed, from Tommy Ice Cream's already mythical kick, the edited highlights in reverse.

There were no assemblies on Fridays. Classes had prayers in their own rooms with their own teachers.

In Miss Palmer's we sat at our desks with hands together and eyes closed. A semi-religious thought somehow smuggled its way into my head. I had spent my Sunday School collection money on a sherbet dip from Milward's. Money from my mother's purse, Dennis Johnson's marbles, God's collection. (Sorry, God.)

Miss Palmer's room was special: it had a slope, a rake like a lecture room or theatre. Leaving your place and standing next to the teacher's desk was like going on stage or entering a bullring. The desks were the usual type, worn and polished wood, black metal, integrated inkwells. There were rows of doubles down the middle and singles down the sides.

Miss Palmer, to be fair, was not a bad teacher. She had a habit, though, of mobilizing the other children against you when work or behaviour was not to her liking.

'What do you think of this, 4A? Hm? Shameful.'

4A. Yes, we were the clever class, supposedly, 11+ candidates: Spencer, Trevor, me; not Joey surprisingly, or Monica more's the pity.

My memories of classroom life, the actual lessons and such, have faded. The playground and the park are much more vivid. However, I still possess, found

BOROUGH OF OLDBURY EDUCATION COMMITTEE.

ROOD END PRIMARY SCHOOL.

REPORT FOR HALF YEAR ENDING July 1953

Name Allan Ahlberg   Age 11 1/12 yrs.

Class Form IV A   No. of Children in Class 55

No. of Times Absent 3   No. of Times Late 1

Position in Class 12   Intelligence Test

Subject.	Max. Mk.	Mk. Obt.	Position	Remarks.
Arithmetic	20	17	13	Good.
Mental Arithmetic	20	17	12	Good.
Composition	20	7	39	Poor.
Spelling	20	12	26	V Fair
Writing	20	13	28	Fair.
Reading	20	18	22	V. Good
Recitation	20	15	11	V Fair
Geography	20	16	16	Good.
History	20	20	1	Excellent
Elem. Science	20	17	8	Good.
Art	20	16	16	Good.
Needle Work	-	-	-	
Craft	20	6	44	V. Poor
Scripture	20	17	17	Good.
P.T.	-	3		Fair

GENERAL REMARKS. Allan could do much better work. He is most inattentive and dreamy at times

Class Teacher's Signature B. Palmer.   *Head Teacher's Signature* E. J. Reynolds

Parent's Signature Mrs Ahlberg

in that box of my mother's things, a slim green folder. It has my best eleven-year-old's writing on the front. *School Reports,* it says, and my name. And here it all is: number of times absent, number of times late. Subjects – marks obtained – position in class. General remarks, 'Inattentive and dreamy at times'. My mother's clumsy signature at the bottom.

The subjects we were taught in those days included the usual: Arithmetic, Spelling, Reading, Composition. Miss Palmer, I see, placed me 39th in the class for Composition: marks obtained, 7 out of 20. Oh dear, and here I am now writing, *composing* a whole book. And she's in it.

One *un*usual subject was Recitation. For Recitation you had to learn a poem, stand beside the teacher's desk and recite it to her. Spencer, I remember, despite his shyness, was brilliant at this:

> My room's a square and candle-lighted boat,
> In the surrounding depths of night afloat.
> My windows are the portholes, and the seas
> The sound of rain on the dark apple-trees.
>
> Frances Cornford

I wasn't bad myself, it seems: position in class 11th; marks obtained, 15 out of 20. Of course, all my best subjects were missing from these reports. *Alibis*: marks obtained, 20 out of 20. *Climbing Trees*: position in class, top.

Playtime came and we returned to more important matters.

'If y'picked a team . . .' Spencer was developing a line of thought.

'That penalty!' So was I.

'The best players . . .'

'It's called a double bluff!'

'From their team and our team . . .'

'See, I really fooled 'im.'

'You'd be in it.'

Spencer had my attention. The combined best team, it was an interesting idea.

'Joey'd be in it,' I said.

'Him too.'

'Tommy Pye!'

'Tommy Ice Cream.'

'Wyatt!'

How peculiar. There was I thinking how could we have won, when all the while the bigger, better question was, how could we have lost? Five of us, and Tommy Pye was the best of the best, and Tommy Ice Cream the biggest of the best. They had Vincent the Invincible, Amos, a whirlwind of fearless muscle,

Tommy Gray, Rutter, Higgsy. And we had . . .

'It was the team,' said Spencer.

In the afternoon we had craft as usual with Mr Cork. I was useless at craft: 6 out of 20, position in class 44th. Dad's dexterity had gone south in my case, down into my feet. The boys in Mr Cork's class (4B) had warned us what to expect. The days of shaking Wyatt's hand were dead and buried.

'Ahlberg, penalty king – c'mere.'

Later on, in the warmth of the classroom, the sun shining in through high church-like windows, Mr Cork, with a practised wriggling action, removed his coat. The shirt sleeve of his missing arm was pinned up. The thought of that never-to-be-seen stump fascinated us. And the gone-forever arm. There was a rumour once he had a finger of it still, a souvenir complete with signet ring, pickled in a jar. And how did he tie his shoelaces, we wondered, or carve the Sunday roast?

During afternoon play something happened: the first onslaught of events. Amos had a fight with Phippy. It was a theatrical scene even by our standards. Maurice Phipps, son of the park-keeper, was a mild-mannered, skinny-looking, essentially timid boy who for some reason brought out the worst in Amos. Amos was no bully, he'd fight anybody, but something about Maurice maddened him. Anyway, Amos must've been teasing or torturing Maurice, winding him up one way or another, and suddenly he went berserk. His eyes rolled up into his head and, howling like an animal, he hurled himself at his tormentor. Amos struggled to comprehend this attack, swatting at Maurice and throwing punches. But Maurice, in the place he was now in, felt no pain and showed no fear. He was an engine of fists and elbows, knees, feet and, eventually, teeth. He took a lump out of Amos's ear. In an instant there was blood everywhere, as though that earlobe was some kind of cork in Amos which, when removed, let out just about every drop of blood he had. The encircling crowd of kids, another larger animal, howled too. How awful! How savage! We might've stood there unflinching and seen Amos murdered. Only then the teachers arrived, barging their way in, pouring cold water on the crime, dousing the passions. A little kid, from the sight of all that blood, fainted, fell down and cracked *his* skull, or flattened his nose or something. More blood! Eventually, the pair of them were driven off in Mrs Harris's car to the hospital. Amos received four stitches and a tetanus injection.

*

And so to Tugg Street at six o'clock, me with my load of firewood standing outside Starkey's and *Vincent Loveridge* approaching. Vincent had been to the hospital too, had the day off from school, stitches for him as well in that cut above his eyebrow. And he came on with his little sister beside him, legs whizzing to keep up. Vincent, the Lord of the School, who never before had even – even slightly – noticed my existence. Came on, drew level, nodded and spoke.

'How y'doin'?'

I think I made a wry face, indicating my heavy, cumbersome sack, and nodded in return, but said nothing, a mumble maybe. And he went on then, and so did I. And it was the best part.

19

The Worm Bank

Four days to the final.

On Saturday morning I escaped Mum's timetable of jobs – bed-making, chamberpot-emptying – and disappeared up the park with Spencer. I'd pay for it later, but it was worth it. We set up a goal against the high hedge at the back of the bowling green and practised penalties, free kicks and so on. Spencer was a hopeless goalie, but willing. We did a bit of dribbling, acting out the pages of *The Stanley Matthews Football Book*, complete with commentary.

There was an uncertainty about Spencer's movements – I can picture him now – an awkwardness, as I perfected my matadorial side-step: moving left, moving left, inside of the foot, outside of the foot – darting right! It was a mystical business, almost zen-like: add your opponent's speed to yours, steal it from him, so to speak, and you become . . . a blur.*

On the way out, circling the pond, we encountered Mr Skidmore. He was sitting on a folding stool, fishing. Mr Skidmore had all the gear – rods, nets, basket. We peered into his keep net to admire a couple of gudgeon swimming around. He hired us to get him a few worms.

The worm bank was a kind of ancient compost heap, added to from time to time by the park gardeners. A secret, humid place, a tropical bubble, surrounded by rhododendron bushes. It was beloved by boys and fishermen, and home to a particular breed of thin red worm perfect for catching anything from sticklebacks to pike. I'm exaggerating again.

Spencer and I took Mr Skidmore's worm tin and

* *Spencer on Ice.* Another picture, even as I write this, *slides* into my mind. (There are many pictures, innumerable pictures.) This one has Spencer poised in all his vulnerable stiffness in the playground, in the winter, in the snow and frosty air, on the ice.

> Others approach more cautiously;
> Denis for one (though he wouldn't agree).
> His wobbly style is unmistakable:
> The sign of a boy who knows he's breakable.
>
> *The Mighty Slide* (1988)

For Denis read Spencer.

went digging. Spencer was in a speculative mood.

'These worms could've dug through from the cemetery, y'know.'

The boundary fence was right behind us.

'Worms don't dig.'

'Burrowed, then. It's not far.'

'It is for a worm.'

'A flea can jump fifteen times its own height.'

'Put the tin down there.'

I added a handful of worms to the wriggling mass. Spencer took up the tin again and gazed thoughtfully into it.

'Who'd be a worm?' he wondered.

At the park gates going out we met Tommy Pye and brother Albert coming in. They had Tommy's brand-new puppy with them on a lead. The four of us proceeded to play with the puppy, recently christened Ramona, encouraging it to chase us, roll around with us, muck us up with its muddy paws, lick our faces. The plump little thing grew dizzy from all this attention.

Back in the street, Spencer and I explored the phenomenon of prodigies in the Pye family. Tommy, yes, what a player! But Albert, it looked like, was promising to be even better. Moreover, Mrs Pye, we'd heard and could more or less see, was expecting her third. What kind of player would that baby be? Probably got a good kick on him even now.

'Yeah.' I grabbed Spencer in a headlock. 'Better than you and he's not even born.'

We made our way up Rood End Road to Lavender's Bread Shop, bought a couple of penny buns, compliments of Mr Skidmore, and sat eating them on the chapel steps. I was reluctant to go home, though I knew I had to. I was steeling myself. We contemplated the scene: people and prams, bikes, motorbikes, buses, the occasional car. Life in those days, I realize now, was the complete set, the perfect jigsaw (though a 'puzzle' still, as always). Walking those streets, in that weather at that time, each piece – Archie, old man Cutler, Mrs Milward (anxious face at the window) – was easily familiar to me, as were the fences, front doors, dusty hedges, gutters and drains, even the flagstones themselves, which I go back and walk on now, fifty years later. And puppies (and babies) arrived to claim their places, become familiar in their turn, grow old and die. Organic, that's what it was, a tangle of lives, like worms in a worm tin.

We went home. As it turned out, Mum was in a reasonable mood. She was standing at the front door with a mop in her hand, talking to Spencer's mum. Spencer said hallo to my mum, so I said hallo to his. It was a funny thing; Spencer really admired my mum. I think he liked the fact that she could fight all the other mothers with one arm tied behind her. She was a dangerous woman, but would stick up for you when the chips were down. And I liked his. She was a terrible snob, but I noticed how often she spoke well of Spencer, praised him; his accordion playing, his cooking, his overall appearance. On the rare occasion I attempted to dress up and look smart, my mother described me as 'a bag of shite tied up in the middle'. I sometimes think we should've swapped.

In the afternoon we met up with Ronnie, running an errand for his gran. We accompanied him to the butcher's. Ronnie bought a pound of sausages and a couple of pounds of scrag-end. I stared at, could not take my eyes off, the poor little skinned rabbits – 'Bye Baby Bunting, Daddy's gone a-hunting' – hanging up by their front, still-furry paws from a row of hooks on a rail in the window.

Ronnie was in no hurry to return home with his shopping. We went back to the park. Tony Leatherland and some others were kicking a ball about in the swings; a couple of rowers were out on the pond; Mr Skidmore was fishing still. Ronnie was keen to conduct an experiment with an earwig. It was generally believed, by us kids anyway, that if an earwig got into your ear (and why else call it an earwig?), it could travel from there to your brain and send you mad. Ronnie hoped to obtain an earwig and thereafter, I suppose, an ear (not his own).

If Tommy Pye was a natural, Ronnie Horsfield was a naturalist, a great gazer into muddy puddles, grassy banks and hedgerows, a lifter-up of rotting logs and corrugated-iron sheeting. Ants' nests and frogspawn held a fascination for him. He would climb any tree if there was a nest in it. But Ronnie was a boy with a reputation. He blew frogs up with a straw. There, I've said it! There was other stuff too, involving fledgling birds etc. He was reported to cut the heads off sticklebacks. But it was the frog story that got to everybody. Frogs fascinated Ronnie and I guess he fascinated us. There again, I cannot say I ever witnessed him do any of this. He never spoke or boasted of it. It was just said of him that he did these things. It was his reputation.

Ronnie found no earwigs that day, it was the wrong time of year, but he did share a bit of his gran's scrag-end with Archie, inviting him to perform a three-legged leap for it. And he would've shared one of his sausages with us. He wanted us to get a fire going in the bushes and cook it. We tried begging matches from a couple of fishermen (Mr Skidmore had departed), but had no luck. Thus Ronnie's grandma's sausages survived and he took them home.

Four days to the final – well, three and a half now. A practice match had been arranged by Spencer, with Leatherland's lot again, for Monday after school. Tuesday too, probably. As for Wednesday, that depended on the unpredictable Mr Cork. Would he be marching us down to GKN's ground as usual, have us running around for an hour and a half *before* the final? You wouldn't put it past him.

One other worry we had, looking ahead to the final itself, was: the shirts. Spencer had received a letter giving details of various presentations, speeches and so on. The teams would get to shake hands with the Mayor and Mayoress of Oldbury, Alderman and Mrs Haywood of Haywood's Outfitters fame. How well did they know their own stock, we wondered? Were they liable to recognize it, if it shook hands with them? We'd find out soon enough.

20

Lucky and Unlucky Omens

Accles & Pollock made weldless steel tubes of every kind and for every purpose, right the way down in size to hypodermic needles. There was a story told, and popularly believed in Oldbury, that in the 1930s an American steel-tube manufacturer sent Accles & Pollock a sample of their finest-diameter tube, claiming it as 'the smallest in the world'. The grimed and sweaty men of Oldbury had a good look at it and, eventually, sent it back with one of their own inside it.

Accles's sports ground was up on the Wolverhampton Road. We needed a bus to get there. There were fourteen of us, all told: the team, plus Spencer, Brenda and Patrick Prosser with his well-autographed if grubby plaster cast. We charged upstairs to the smoke-filled upper deck. Normally, the conductor would have put a stop to this, but we had him outnumbered. Tommy Pye instantly went into a panic, claiming he had lost his fare. He found it almost immediately, in his hand. Ronnie had to be dissuaded from hiding under a seat to avoid paying his. There was a scramble to occupy the front seats, a constant barrage of yelling. You'd think we were mountaineers communicating across a valley. Only Tommy Ice Cream was quiet and, temporarily, Wyatt, consuming a pork pie.

'Read it again!' yelled Joey.

Spencer, looking smart in a jacket and tie, took out the letter from the Parks and Cemeteries department.

'Which bit?'

'Read about the presentations!'

'The medals!'

'Ray Barlow!'

'Right,' said Spencer, a little wearily. 'It says here, "On the conclusion of the contest –" '

'Contest?'

'*Con*test?'

' "Of the contest, players and officials alike –" '

'Hey, look – an ambulance!'

In those days an ambulance (and a million other things) was considered an unlucky omen unless responded to with the appropriate ritual.

'Touch y'collar!'
'Touch y'collar!'
'Don't swallow till y'see a dog!'
'"Players and officials –"'
'Aren't you 'ot in that?'
Ronnie in his balaclava makes no reply.
'"Will assemble in two parallel lines on the –"'
'A dog.'
'A dog!'
'Another dog!'
'If we win –'
'*When* we win.' Ronnie (naturally).

'When we win.' This was Edna May, looking, I have to report, rather fetching in a Fair Isle bobble hat and with a gap-toothed smile. She had lost a tooth from a smack in the face from the ball in the semi-final. 'Will Spencer make a speech?'

'No,' said Spencer.

'Yes!' yelled half a dozen others.

'*Spotty* dog!' cried Tommy Pye.

A spotty dog was considered to be a lucky omen, needing only to be observed for the luck to stick.

'I could make a speech!' Edna May again.

'Me too!' Brenda.

'Well . . . don't.' This in a menacingly sepulchral voice, suddenly and startlingly from the back of the bus. A large, untidy-looking man with a greyhound between his knees and a cigarette in his mouth was scowling at us. He said no more but we got the message and whispered from then on.

'Trev.'

'What?'

'Trev.'

'What?'

'Show 'em y'leg.'

Cheerfully, proudly, Trevor rolled down his left sock to reveal a lumpy bruise on his shin. Earlier in the day he had collided with, been mown down by is nearer the truth, Nellie Shipman. Nellie Shipman was a cantankerous blind woman who, like Tommy Ice Cream, roamed the streets, though in her case at surprising speed and laying about her with a white stick, connecting in this instance with Trevor's shin. The protests and cries of pain she regularly provoked guided her steps. None of this 'tap, tap' business. A blind man was another lucky omen, but not, it seems, a blind woman. Not Nellie Shipman. Not for Trevor.

The man with the greyhound got off the bus at the Brades. The conductor came up to collect our fares.

'Read it again,' said Joey.

21

Pomegranates

Accles & Pollock's sports ground was situated to the north of the town, an oasis of football and cricket pitches, tennis courts, bowling green, running track, set down in an otherwise blasted landscape of waste tips, slag heaps, marl holes. Tall poplars marked its boundary on the Wolverhampton Road. There was an imposing pair of weldless steel-tube gates, through which at a quarter to six on that Wednesday evening we rowdily and shyly passed.

The pitch itself was amazing, the best we'd ever played on or ever would, most of us. Full size of course, the goalposts too, a ludicrous space for ten- and eleven-year-olds. Not that we minded; the bigger the better. There was a covered stand near the halfway line and other temporary seating set out around the pitch. The sun was clipping the tops of the poplars, projecting their shadows across that huge expanse of grass.

THE OLDBURY AND DISTRICT
QUEEN ELIZABETH II CORONATION
CUP FINAL

ROUNDS GREEN PRIMARY 'A' V.
MALT SHOVEL ROVERS

VENUE: ACCLES & POLLOCK'S
SPORTS GROUND
DATE: 22 APRIL 1953

KICK-OFF: 6.15 P.M.

First half. As I write this now, pen in hand, ink on paper, down the garden in my shed, my hand is shaking (truly), slippery with sweat. I want you to feel it too, all those knotted stomachs in the changing room, that breathless on-the-edgeness. I'd hate you to think it was just some kids kicking a ball.

By the time we stepped out, clattering down the pavilion steps, everybody was there: parents, kids, dogs, dignitaries. I spotted Mr Reynolds sitting in the stand, and Mr Glue looking, with one black eye . . . wary. He'd had a fight, we learnt later, with one of those so-called mates of his. Mr Ash had flitted in and out, wishing us luck. A couple of constables and an inspector, prompting unease in one or two of our more guiltily inclined hearts. No sign of Uncle Ike yet, or Dad. Mum was there, frowning as usual, hat crammed on her head, Dinah on a lead. No offices would get cleaned tonight, not by her anyway.

We won the toss, lined up and kicked off, stitching passes up the field:

Ronnie to me –

me to Arthur –

to Trevor –

to me again –

ball inside the full back –

Wyatt –

loping stride and dipping shoulder –

lovely left foot –

goal.

Goal! Thirty seconds flat and their lot hadn't touched it. The crowd was stunned. There were more of their supporters than ours, Rounds Green being just down the hill, not half a mile away. Anyway, what a start! Our faces shone like beacons in the oddly luminous (but locally familiar) light that was already enveloping the ground. We were winning and could end up winning. Why not? Why ever not?

And yet . . .

There was something, something peculiar, a sense of strangeness that many of us felt even before we had any reason to feel it.

It could've been the light. (British Summer Time

was operating now, by the way. The clocks had been put forward, transferring an extra hour of daylight to the end of the day.) Accles's beautiful ground was an oasis all right, but the surrounding nether regions did not give up that easily. Slag heaps and waste tips, hardly two hundred yards away, steamed and puckered like hot swamps in the daytime and glowed in the night. Radioactivity could not be ruled out.*

It could've been the crowd, which though large enough for a crowd was too polite, too subdued somehow, to actually be one. Intimidated, perhaps, by the formality of the seating and the presence of dignitaries.

But, no, not the crowd, not the light. The strangeness was, well, it took some working out, but here's a clue: this is *their* first goal, scored as they lined up and kicked off after our first goal:

pass –
run into space –
ball to feet –

* There has been much in the papers lately (2004) about the Huygens space probe visiting Titan, one of the moons of Saturn. Much can be learnt, apparently, about the atmosphere of the early Earth by studying Titan's atmosphere. Well, all I can say is, come back to Oldbury in 1953; there's the early Earth for you: all the sulphur, methane and ammonia you could ever wish for.

pass –
run –
dip the shoulder –
lovely right foot –
goal.

And our lot never touched it. That was the peculiar, the disconcerting thing (like all those Ackerman faces in the semi-final): *the similarities between the teams*. They played their football the way we played ours, held their positions, passed it around and so on. But it didn't stop there. They had a big goalie, a beanpole of a boy, as tall as Tommy Ice Cream if not as wide. They had a Tommy Pye as well, a tiny little golden-curled eight-year-old named Sammy Turpin, who all the mothers once again instantly felt protective towards. They howled disapproval if we went anywhere near him.

The match proceeded in its increasingly symmetrical fashion, like a chess game, each side confronting the other with itself. They even had an offside trap. It was like playing in front of a mirror. It was a good game, even so. The pitch was flat and true, and considering our ages and inexperience, we played well, all eleven – no, be fair – all twenty-two of us.

When half-time arrived it was 3–2 to them.

Families and friends gathered about us. Mr Skidmore, Uncle Ike and Mrs Prosser sought to give us the benefit of their advice. My mum, always uncomfortable in company and away from her own doorstep, approached, gave me a hopeful half-smile, but didn't speak. Dad had yet to arrive. Tommy Ice Cream, meanwhile, was astounding everybody by sounding off to Joey and Trevor. His vocabulary had continued to expand. 'Kickit!' and 'Shoo!' he explained. And sometime later, 'Gol!' (goal) and 'Spenceth!' (Spencer says).

With half-time almost over, Rufus rolled up (no Albert) in an overcoat and a trilby hat, carrying a crumpled bag full of – wait for it – pomegranates.

I know, I know, unbelievable, but it happened. Anyway, oranges were rare enough in those days, so why not pomegranates? Rufus cut them up into halves and quarters and I suppose thereafter we . . . ate 'em. I can vaguely remember eating pomegranates back then, buying the odd one from Bastable's on the way home from the grammar school. You ate them – yes, I do remember it – you ate them, like cockles and whelks, with a pin. But there we are, that was it, the final flourish, the last exotic cherry on that luminously glowing, mirror-imaged cake. Pomegranates.

*

Second half. Spencer took up his position behind Tommy Ice Cream's goal, directing Tommy's siege-gun kicks and mighty overarm throws. Tommy Pye and Sammy Turpin squared up in midfield, dribbled each other, tackled each other, bowled each other over like a pair of bantams. (The watching mothers were dumbstruck, I'll bet, not knowing who to yell for, or at.) And they scored, a long-range shot in off the bar; and we scored, a long-range courageous diving bullet header from Joey. And Wyatt chatted with the crowd. And Ronnie argued with the ref. And they scored.

Our stars were the usual: Tommy Pye and Wyatt in attack, Joey in defence. But others of us shone that evening, and all of us worked our socks off. I'd like to give a special mention to Arthur and Edna May. Arthur was an unshowy player, cool and understated. He tackled people, got the ball and calmly fed it on to Wyatt or me. Made no fuss. Ran into space. Passed it.

And Edna May: Edna May had easily her best game. It helped, I suspect, that the full back marking her – with an extra flush to his freckled cheeks? – was clearly smitten. (He had a tooth missing too.) She was alert from the start, up for it. And brave; would sacrifice more teeth if she had to. Like Arthur, she did the simple things, no fuss.

You almost forgot she was a girl. And then, the not-so-simple: showing up on the left wing, to Wyatt's consternation (and their right back's), setting Wyatt free, his blinding shot then ricocheting around the goal mouth, to be bundled in at last, or neatly tucked away I rather should have said, by me.

The pace was frantic; we sped across that vast pitch like pocket dynamos, pink-faced in the pink light, damp hair plastered to our boiling heads. And the crowd was a real crowd now, roaring and boiling themselves. Mrs Glue was there (with Mr), and my dad, dirty-faced from work. Ice Cream Jack in his long brown overall of a coat had materialized next to Spencer. The tall blond god-like figure of Ray Barlow himself was standing up in the stand. A great game – oh yes! – and a memorable time, seared forever into our brains and pounding hearts. Joyful and dazzling. Oh yes . . .

Pity about the result.

22

Shaking Hands with Ray Barlow

We could've won, should've won and nearly did. Hit the bar – denied a penalty – they were hanging on at the end. There again, they did hang on and we didn't win. There again (again!), 'Yeth and noth', we did win. Sort of. Y'see, when you come to think about it, and I'm not just saying this because we lost, the *semi*-final was our final. Beating Amos and Vincent Loveridge, showing Mr Cork. Rising up out of the bottom pitch. Doing it on our own. Getting a team up.

The final was fantastic, win or lose; the crowd cheering, having our photo taken for the *Weekly News*, shaking hands with Ray Barlow. *Shaking hands with Ray Barlow!* Getting our medals, and treasuring them still, some of us, in their shiny golden cardboard boxes. Showing them off to our mums and dads, uncles, sisters, dogs. Tremendous, all of it. But for sure, the semi-final was the thing, the big event, the glow that has lingered, in my mind anyway, down all these years.

As for the shirts, no problem. Alderman and Mrs Haywood greeted us, one and all, shaking our grubby hands and smiling. Of course, their valuable stock, if it was their stock, had undergone a transformation in the past few weeks: dyed and shrunk up, tailored, singed. Its own mother wouldn't have known it. Nevertheless, for some of us melodrama still ruled.

''E *looked* at me.'

'And me!'

'What else d'you expect?'

'Yeah – he's shakin' y'hand.'

'Otherwise you'd miss each other!'

'Shake somebody else's.'

'Reynolds's!'

'Ray Barlow's!'

'The ref's!'

'All the same, 'e looked.'

I caught sight of Tommy Ice Cream's face, round and moon-like, wondering. His medal flat out on the palm of his hand. And I recalled him shaking hands in his turn with all of them, solemn and attentive, thinking to himself . . . what? What was he thinking? I've no idea.

Then, '*I* looked at *'im*,' said Ronnie.

*

We left the ground in fading light, its luminosity snuffed out but with a greenish tinge condensing yet around the street lamps. Out on the driveway beyond the imposing gates a pony and cart was waiting. The silvery gleam of a milk churn in the back of the cart caught our collective eye. Ice creams were served by the silent but hospitable Ice Cream Jack, real name, I've lately discovered, Giuseppe. The cornets that we got that night, doubles and triples, lasted us half the way home as we waited patiently at the bus stop or walked on impatiently to the next. The crowd of us plus family and friends gradually broke up into smaller clusters, pairs, individuals. The night closed in. Plumes of smoke from the brickworks' chimneys rose up into the sky. The underside of clouds threw back a radiant glow from Danks's furnaces. Dinah tugged me along, urgently to nowhere in particular, the next stop. I finished my ice cream.

PS I meant to end this chapter here, but suddenly realized – Ray Barlow! You won't know who he is, was (is?). Ray Barlow was a prince among footballers, the elegant left half for West Bromwich Albion. In those days WBA were the top team in the land. Exaggerating? Not at all. They won the

FA Cup and very nearly did the double. Maybe in recent times, the last forty years or so, other upstart teams, Man United, Chelsea, have popped up to challenge their position, but it's only temporary. Take my word, we'll be back. Anyway, Ray Barlow, an ace player, gracing the Hawthorns with his cool, unflustered play. As boys in those more robust times, we often found ourselves passed down, like rolls of carpet, over the heads of the 40–50,000 cloth-capped crowd to the front of the stands, to stand with our noses barely above the parapet, with a perfect view . . . of the players' ankles. Ray Barlow's elegant ankles.

Part Two

23

Resting Where No Shadows Fall

It was the blackest day (smother amid smother), yet it began so well. Spencer came round. 'Look,' he said. 'Thruppence!' He had picked it up off the pavement outside.

'I dropped that!' I declared, turning my pockets out and frowning.

'No,' said Spencer.

Mum gave us each a stick of rhubarb and some sugar in a twist of paper. We left for the park. It was August now, school holidays, a baking thunderous day already and it was only half past eight. In the street we passed a doubly shaky Mrs Moore shaking somebody's hand. Monica Copper was in her garden. I gave Spencer a shove and started running as we went by.

One thing about Spencer, which you might not have guessed from his shy manner, was he liked to talk. (I was different. Conversation did not flourish in our house. I had more to say to Dinah.) When we played with Spencer's Dinkys and soldiers, he kept up a running commentary: 'You and your men are coming down this road. Me and my men are round this corner. You hear a horse!' When fishing, he watched me more than his float, and talked.

Now, in the park, by the pond, on the swings, in the hollow tree behind the boathouse – him in it, me up it – Spencer promoted a steady exchange of thought and feeling. What did I prefer, jam or lemon curd? How many sneezes might there have been around the planet in a single day, or in World History even? How should he spend his thruppence?

At the worm bank, assisting little Albert Pye digging for his dad, Spencer contemplated the degrees of life in a man, or a cat, say – a spider – a worm. Suddenly, he fell silent, cocking his head on one side like a bird.

'Listen, y'can hear 'em.'

I assumed he was pulling my leg. Little Albert, however, paused in his work and cocked *his* head, though he was more or less at ground level anyway. And there it was, the tiniest sound, a dry rustling in the leaf mould: worms on the move.

*

At Lavender's Spencer bought two iced buns for a penny. With his remaining tuppence he bought a packet of transfers from Milward's. We returned to the park, eating the buns and sticking the transfers on our arms.

Spencer said, 'My cousin used to tell me, don't be scared 'cos God's at the end of the bed.'

'Whose bed?'

'Everybody's. And that got me puzzled. I used to think, well, there must be lots of gods.'

'Probably are.'

'No, I think there's just one and he gets everywhere. Sort of splits up.'

We broke off then to pursue a butterfly with Spencer's coat. Yes, coat; his mother wrapped him up even in that heat.

Spencer said, 'I argue with my cousin. I say, "Do you believe in God?" and he says, "Yes!" and I say, "Well, how did *he* start?" Because what puzzles me is, if God was the first person in the Universe, who made him?'

We were lying back on the parched grass. I could still see the distant wavering butterfly.

Spencer said, 'What gets me is, there couldn't have been anything in the world then. It must've been . . . just plain sky.'

*

The flow of time is slower when you're a child. April seen from August was a lifetime off, Accles & Pollock's the other side of the moon, and the team ancient history. As for the Coronation, well, it took place, I suppose, but I have nothing to say about it. On the day itself I went fishing with Uncle Ike. Anyway, this is not a book about queens and princes, as you may have spotted.

After the final and the Easter holidays, we returned to school and, lo and behold, the cricket season was upon us. But though the game was different, the circumstances were the same: Mr Cork and sixty-six boys – Guest, Keen & Nettlefold's – wickets, bats and balls, plus, if you were lucky, a pad or two – the top pitch and the bottom. Mr Cork's imagination was limited. His chosen footballers simply became his chosen cricketers. When you were in, you were in. Down on the bottom pitch, lumpy and unmown, teams were picked, but mainly chaos ruled. Some poor beleaguered batsman would attempt to score while a multitude of fielders, half of 'em his own team, did their best to prevent him. And no umpire.

So Malt Shovel Rovers roved no more. A few of us (fanatics) still played football through the summer, others joined Leatherland's lot for cricket matches in the park. Edna May had no interest in cricket but could often be found cycling around the boundary edge in Joey Skidmore's vicinity. Tommy Ice Cream . . . Tommy was no cricketer either, though occasionally he'd have a go. In the summer term he put in a surprise appearance on the first morning, sitting down in Mrs Belcher's class as if he'd never been away. He would lumber over and stand near Spencer in the playground, swing a leg at a ball if it came near him. I saw his dad once, watching anxiously at the gates. But none of it lasted. Tommy stopped coming to school after barely a week. He resumed his wayward patrol of the streets, retreated again, disappearing down into that monstrous coat he ever and always wore.

In the afternoon, after a hurried sandwich and glass of milk at Spencer's, and accompanied now by Ronnie, we found ourselves in the cemetery. No, not 'accompanied' – led. Ronnie liked to go to places where he shouldn't, or wasn't, wanted, the railway line, for instance, or the allotments. It pleased him to exercise his rights. He had a right to go into the cemetery whatever the superintendent said. His grandma paid her taxes; his uncle, a stonemason, carved the graves.

The heat of the day by now was stifling. The

sky, stuffed full and stained by all the smokestacks of Oldbury, had baked itself to a golden brown.

Ronnie poked and pried among the graves, looking for wildlife. The gravediggers had been cutting the grass, raking it into huge sweet-smelling piles, too tempting altogether not to take running leaps into. There were graves that had with time collapsed in on themselves, gone crooked, gaping open. We craned our necks and grazed our knees in search of coffins . . . bodies . . . bones. Spencer read aloud from various headstones: 'Resting where no shadows fall . . . be ye also ready . . . safe in the arms of Jesus'. One stone in particular fascinated him. He had read it before on a previous visit: 'In loving memory of Gordon, dear son of F. E. and F. E. Percy, died October 22 1948, aged 5 years. Dead! Nay, safe in God's home port, he is not dead. Also his auntie, Ivy Muriel Lowe, died July 6 1950, aged 26'.

There were heart-shaped stones and stones like open books. Stone angels of various shapes and sizes, innumerable crosses.

We wandered up to the main gates and took a drink of water from the tap. The superintendent, I forget his name, came out of his house in time to catch a scowl from Ronnie and watch us leave.

Back in the park we did a bit of climbing, up

one tree and down the other, a favourite routine. Ronnie used his penknife to cut trapdoors in the grass and hide things: a marble, cigarette packet, bus ticket. Parents with little kids – pushchairs and ice creams – zombied by, dazed in the heat. Perspiring rowers circled the pond. We sat on the grass, panting like dogs, and watched a cricket match: Joey, Trevor, Tony Leatherland, etc. A fourth dog, an altogether cooler dog, Archie, sat with us for a while, sniffed around, moved on. Suddenly, a fight erupted, Joey and Arthur. We leapt up and moved closer. The two of them were tangled together like an octopus, rolling around, pinning each other down, throwing punches. Once again, as usual, a primitive, pitiless circle formed of fellow cricketers and other kids; spectators, witnesses, accomplices.

It was a short fight and a brave one. But Joey was the bigger, harder boy. Arthur had a bloody nose, his face was smeared with blood and tears and snot, his shirt all grass-stained and bloody too, and torn. I might have spoken or gone off with him when he left, but it was all so fast. And there was Joey too, with a great scratch all down his arm, and bloodied likewise, his own and Arthur's. Then Leatherland set up the stumps again and the game resumed. A mother and her little girl prepared to fly a home-made kite. We thought of heading off to the water fountain or the café even, for a drink. The brown crust of the sky darkened above us.

24

The Tree

Piling on. This is done either 'to hurt a person if he has done wrong', after he has been forcibly thrown to the ground, or, as opportunity occurs, during rough play, when somebody accidentally falls, and one of the company jumps on top of him, yelling 'Pile on', a summons readily obeyed by everybody else rushing up and adding their weight on top of the fallen one.

The Chamber. 'One boy is put between the door and the wall, then damp leaves are thrown over him.' – Boy, 13, Laindon, Essex.

Iona and Peter Opie,
The Lore and Language of Schoolchildren (1959)

I was afraid of many things in those days, including my own mother. I was afraid of Amos in the playground, the ghost in the boathouse, the Toomeys

– oranges and pomegranates notwithstanding – everywhere. I did not like the dark on the landing or the man in the mac with the livid scar down the side of his neck who sometimes walked his dog up Cemetery Road. I was afraid of the cemetery in general and the gravediggers' hut in particular. This did not prevent me from sneaking in at times, in the half-dark, in search of nests or even for a dare. I taught myself to swim in the canal, yet still I had a fear of drowning. A boy I slightly knew caught his foot in a submerged bedstead jumping in off Tipton Bridge. They did not recover his body for three or four hours. I was afraid of horseflies, which, since I believed their sting could kill a horse, they surely could kill me.

There *was* more violence towards children. Mr Reynolds with his cane, other teachers slapping the tender backs of little infants' legs. Mothers slapped their children stingingly around the head, 'clipped their ears'. Dads came home from work and hit them with a belt when it was called for, usually by the mothers. More violence, yes, but not necessarily less love. Things in those days were just more, what's the word? Well, just more. Don't judge us all too harshly; it was normal enough.

*

The Toomeys came after us about half an hour later, the brothers that is, all seven of them, including Arthur. A hunting party – their ages ranged from nine to nineteen – thirsting for revenge. They were a tribe all right. Hit one Toomey and you hit them all. You half expected Mr and Mrs to be out there, and the baby. A tough family, the toughest. And tough on each other. Arthur probably took more punishment in his own house than ever he got elsewhere. But that, of course, was not the point.*

Well, they tracked us down, flushed us out and beat us up. Joey, naturally, was the main target. Leatherland was heavily implicated, it being his bat and ball. The other players, spectators, but really once the Toomeys' blood was up, *anybody*. They threw Trevor in the brook who had been in the toilets when the fight took place. Beat Charlie Cotterill up, out in the street, who was never even in the park. And came then after us, and what had we ever done? But, as I said, the Toomeys' cauldron of anger, outrage, loyalty, vengeance,

* *Total number of Toomeys.* There were two other brothers, as it happened, one married, one in Winson Green prison. Together with the baby, also a boy, that made . . . ten. Ten brothers, two parents, three grandparents, thirty-something uncles, aunts and cousins. Grand total, as anyone might reasonably conclude: too many.

honour was boiling over and their blood was up.

They came at speed in through the gates, loping like wolves, predatory, drooling (!). All the same, you'd think we could've escaped: that vast expanse of shrubberies and trees and grass. We had dens and hiding places all over that park. Rhododendron bushes that created perfect secluded caves of greenery; trees that hung down to the ground like wigwams. Unfortunately, if we knew them, so did the Toomeys.

The grown-ups, incidentally, were no use at all. It never occurred to us to involve them anyway. When you left your house in those days, you were on your own. The adult world was another, parallel universe. Also, in this case, rain was threatening and the families, rowers, fishermen and so on were rapidly departing.

We ran and scattered, split up, hid. I found a place, a narrow ditch in the bushes half filled with last year's leaves and overhung by brambles. It cost me no end of scratches and scrapes to get in there, and torn trousers, but once in I was invisible. Then what? I could hear footsteps on the nearby path, the splash of an oar, the grizzling of an unhappy toddler. What had *he* got to cry about? The occasional fat spot of rain penetrated the canopy and reverberated in the brambles over my head. I was *so* hot, hot with the weather's heat and my own fear. Sweat ran down into my eyes. I quivered and shook like Mrs Moore, like the three little pigs and the wolf, or Bambi and the hunters. And yet – how odd! – I was excited too. It was like the games I'd played for half my life, hiding and seeking, chasing and being caught. And anyway here I was, the invisible boy. They'd never find *me.*

I listened again, ever more intently, holding my breath, hearing . . . incomprehensible shouts and other noises, running feet, my own blood concussing away in my ears. How long was I there? My legs had gone to sleep and were prickled now by tremendous pins and needles (and holly leaves). I urgently needed a piddle. What time was it? It was getting darker. I could not hear a thing. I came out, stepped out on to the path beside the empty rain-bombarded pond. And Ronnie was there, being punched in the stomach by Kenny Toomey. I turned to run. Rufus, like an Indian brave, stepped out of the trees and grabbed me.

The Toomeys preferred a moving target, one they could chase after, pile on and flatten. They liked you to fight back or plead for mercy. But Ronnie was doubled up and I was dumbstruck.

'Stand up!'

'Yeah!'

'Put y'hands on y'head!'

'Yeah, yeah!'

'Do it!'

'Yeah!'

(Punch.)

They smacked me around the head a couple of times, barley-sugared both my arms and shoved me back into the brambles. Ronnie was sick then all over Kenny's shoes, which was some consolation.

And that was it. The Toomeys' punitive expedition had run its course. They'd probably forgotten by now whatever it was had got them roused up in the first place. They left, righteous and weary from their hot exertions, the family's reputation restored.

But if the Toomeys' fever had passed, ours was just beginning, though we scarcely knew it. My mouth was throbbing: I had bitten my own tongue. Angry red spots stood out on Ronnie's otherwise sickly face. The pain of it, the shame of it. We stumbled around for a while unable to look each other in the eye. The infection of revenge was taking hold. *Somebody* had to pay.

We found Spencer sitting alone in the sheds. He was soaking wet but otherwise unharmed. He had been hiding out in the Bandstand Café for nearly an hour with a cup of tea. They never spotted him. Spencer didn't boast of this and showed real concern for our pain and injuries. And, after all, he'd only achieved what we ourselves had tried and failed to do. But we resented him, blamed him, all the same.

The tree grew out at an angle from a grassy bank. Some kind of willow, I suppose, enormous. Its bark was a greyish green. A network of grooves and ridges, like screwed-up paper, provided excellent grip for climbers. Because of the angle and the bank, for the first few feet you could almost walk up it. Higher up it branched out and up, and up again, way out even beyond the boundary of the park itself, hanging up and over the allotments.

'Let's have a climb,' said Ronnie.

Ronnie *was* the cruel one, but I can't offload this on to him. There's no alibi there, it was both of us. Yes, cajoling, teasing, insulting – 'C'mon, c'mon, y'sissie!' – we got Spencer up the tree. He was sad and silent, but he climbed; Ronnie before him, me after. Ronnie was a clever climber, agile and fearless. We were a pair, could climb up almost anything. More to the point, we could climb down it as the need arose, another skill entirely.

Normally, from up in that tree you could see for miles. But today – what *time* was it? – it was like night, a brown and flooded night. Even as we entered the leafier spaces of the tree, a torrent of water was surging down the trunk. The rain like liquid rust, the sky washed clean, transferring its stains to our shirts and skins.

It was a joke at first, we told ourselves, Ha, ha! Getting down and out of the tree, urging Spencer to follow suit, seeing him stuck there. There was so much rain, like a beaded curtain before our eyes. Spencer up high in the branches was invisible almost; a patch of jacket, a smudge of face. We took a step or two along the path, calling to him. And a step or two more. And there was no sign of him now. (Oh, Spencer, my best true friend, what did I do?)

And we left him.

That night there was a knock at the back door. Dad opened it and presently came up and got me out of bed and brought me down to the kitchen. I was rubbing my eyes, bemused with sleep, half wondering where I was. Mr Sorrell, soaking wet, his dripping hat held in his hand, was hovering in the doorway. He was looking for Spencer. Had I seen Spencer? They could not find him. I said something. We had been playing in the park. I had come home. I could not *believe* he was still up in the tree. Well, he wasn't; around that time he was four or five miles away in the Dudley Guest Hospital. Later on, the story came out. How old man Cutler, madly working his swamp of an allotment, or smoking in his shed more like, had heard a sound, seen something.

Spencer had fallen from the tree down on to the spiked railings that separated the park from the allotments. (*Spiked* railings, between a park and a vegetable patch! What in hell were they protecting? Lettuces? Carrots?) Spencer's arm, his left arm, was pierced by one of the spikes. He must have hung there for a while, like one of those rabbits on hooks in the butcher's window. Mr Cutler had got him down and driven him off in his motorbike and sidecar to the hospital. Saved his life, by all accounts, having previously applied a tourniquet, his leather belt, to Spencer's horribly torn and bleeding arm. (There was blood, they said, all down his leg, collecting in his shoe, overflowing it.) Yes, saved his life with that tight tourniquet – hooray for old man Cutler! But lost his arm.

25
Cheltenham

'I've been a bad man.'
Burglar Bill (1977)

The best and the worst of times, and the worst of the worst. A week later I visited Spencer in hospital. Mum came with me on a couple of buses. We took a home-made bread pudding, Spencer loved Mum's bread pudding, and a Dinky toy, my most treasured possession at that time, an American army jeep complete with removable driver.

Spencer sat up in bed in his brand-new Dan Dare pyjamas, one sleeve pinned up. His face was pale, his expression mild, hesitant. Mum said hallo and started crying. She handed over the slab of pudding in its greaseproof-paper wrapping and went outside. I wished she'd stayed. It had not been my idea to come. I was scared and ashamed, embarrassed and almost choked up with guilt. Then Spencer leant towards me and whispered. The boys in the beds on either side of his were both named Spittle! It was a common topic of conversation between us, the troublesome business of names. Any name with 'bottom' in it, for instance – Rowbottom, Sidebottom – was asking for trouble, not to mention Belcher. At the other extreme, the Smiths had named their baby Gerald. He'd suffer for it, in our opinion. Nudge was a name we were amused by, and Tickler. Ahlberg was a dodgy one at times, and, well, *Spencer* . . .

And so we talked and ate some of Spencer's amazing stash of sweets from his bedside locker. Already he had perfected a one-armed technique for removing the wrappers. I needed to say sorry, confess my sins, blame Ronnie! But somehow I was tongue-tied. Spencer made no fuss and was as tactful as ever. I knew he'd told nobody what Ronnie and I – no, *me* and Ronnie – had done. This only left me more conscience-stricken than ever. Spencer, I now believe, climbed that tree (unprotestingly) simply to make amends, accept his share of the suffering, even things up. It was his instinct to do so. And he told no one about it afterwards, or forever as far as I know, because *he* felt guilty.

A nurse came up and gave Spencer some medicine. (A tourniquet, by the way, can be tied too tight, apparently. That's what did it. Plus the infection, dirt and germs from the spiked railings, the rusty rain.) Mum came back with a couple of comics, and soon after we left. She put her arm around my shoulder as we headed off along some endless disinfected corridor. I wriggled free and turned my face so that she could not see it. It was raining when we got outside. Our bus was coming up the hill and we ran to catch it. I never saw Spencer again.

At the beginning of September, we left Cemetery Road, exchanging houses for the last time. My ever-questing mother had found her holy grail, a council semi on Tat Bank Road complete with hot and cold running water, indoor toilet, upstairs bath. There was a patch of garden and permission to keep the hens. It was hardly a mile away from Rood End, the park and all that, but still another world. Yes, she moved me in, my mother, and she moved me out.

And off I went then, up the hill, in a blaze of blazers and ties to Oldbury Grammar School. Ronnie, Joey and the others descended to the Secondary Modern; Spencer, eventually, to another grammar school on the edge of Birmingham, George Dixon's I believe. A new life began, a fresh start, with separate brand-new notebooks for each exotic subject: Algebra, Physics, French! And there were 'houses', Kings, Queens, School, Trinity, and house competitions, sports days, swimming galas. And a school song, and a headmaster in a mortarboard and gown! And girls! Goodbye, Monica Copper; hallo, Norma Finch and Cynthia Richardson.

Our lives, of course, are weaves of lives, aren't they? I don't just mean our parents, brothers, sisters. My life has Mr Cotterill's in it, old man Cutler's, Archie's. Yours, since you are reading this, has mine.

So it ended, or began to end, that boyhood of mine. I became a calmer, more self-contained person, more grown up. I stopped acquiring other people's property, caught myself at it, as it were, even returned a couple of things. In a general way urgency and melodrama subsided. I also became a teenager, it's true, but that's a turmoil of a different kind.

And the years flew by and what became of us?

Tommy Ice Cream worked for his father and,

later on, his sisters, in the shop. Tommy Pye became a moderately famous footballer; Albert Pye a really famous one. Yes, *the* Albert Pye. Rufus and Albert Toomey were in and out of jail, asking for other charges to be taken into consideration, the break-in at Haywood's, I believe, being one of them. Edna May, at eighteen, got married to – would you believe it? – Trevor. I like to imagine him (and her) riding along for the second time in his life, perhaps, in a big posh car. And me? I got a job at Accles's for a while, went in and out of the army (another kind of jail), worked as a postman, plumber's mate, school teacher. And began to write books.

In 1985, I think it was, I was invited to take part in the Cheltenham Literary Festival. I gave a talk to an audience of children and adults, and signed copies of my books afterwards. The queue of people at my signing table was gratifyingly long. I talked to the children, asking them what they'd like me to write, pretending to hold the books upside down, stuff like that. A woman with a pleasant face was standing before me with a boy. He was a medium sort of boy, ten years old perhaps, dark hair combed flat to his head with a knife-like parting; a mild, hesitant expression. It was Spencer.

I half expected him to smell of furniture polish.

But no, it was *Philip*, Spencer's son. They'd heard about me from Spencer, that he and I had known each other thirty years before. (What else had they heard?) He, by the way, had been unable to attend that evening, his wife explained: a parents' evening at the school, where he was head of English. (Did he teach Recitation, I wondered?) He was sorry to have missed me. And I him.

Well, we did talk a few times after that on the phone, and we send each other Christmas cards. But the years keep slipping by, and I still wander the worn-out Oldbury streets from time to time, the paths around the oddly shrunken park, and recollect the goals I scored, and see the tree, which is still there. But we have never met.